A Trusting
Heart

A Trusting Heart

by

Shannon Guymon

BONNEVILLE BOOKS™
Springville, Utah

ISBN: 1-55517-620-8
v.1

Published by Bonneville Books
Imprint of Cedar Fort Inc.
www.cedarfort.com

Distributed by:

Typeset by Kristin Nelson
Cover design by Adam Ford
Cover design © 2002 by Lyle Mortimer

Printed in the United States of America
10 9 8 7 6 5 4 3 2 1

Printed on acid-free paper

Library of Congress Cataloging-in-Publication Data

Guymon, Shannon, 1972-
 A trusting heart / by Shannon Guymon.
    p. cm.
 ISBN 1-55517-620-8
 1. Class reunions--Fiction. I. Title.
 PS3607.U96 T78 2002
 813'.6--dc21

2002006810

To Matt

Chapter 1

Why was she doing this? she asked herself for the tenth time in the last five minutes. She looked down at her shiny, silver polyester skirt she had bought at Wal-Mart just that morning especially for the occasion. It was a good thing polyester had come back in style. It was the only material her bank account approved of. She sighed and tried not to wince. Her Calvin Klein days were long gone. And to think ten years ago, she had taken labels like that for granted. She looked in the mirror one last time. What would they see when they looked at her? How would they label her this time? She wasn't a cheerleader any longer and she wasn't Dylan Carlisle's arm ornament anymore. Maybe there would be no labels this time; maybe they would see her.

Megan Garrett ran the brush through her long honey brown hair and touched up her light makeup. Solemn green eyes stared back at her through the mirror. Ten years ago her eyes had been blue. Her mother's voice echoed through her thoughts, *If you want to be a cheerleader, then you have to look the part. And if you want your father to be proud of you, you'll be a cheerleader.* Megan shook her head to clear away the memories. This was who she was now, and she wouldn't go back to the old Megan Garrett for anything or anyone.

Her classmates probably wouldn't even recognize her! Not that she'd had plastic surgery or been in a disfiguring accident or anything, but take away the blond, permed hair, deep tan, blue contacts and about a pound of makeup, and what was left was a completely different kind of person. Someone she could be proud of. Someone she even kind of liked. The thought stilled her hand. What if she showed up tonight and sat in a corner because no one made the connection between the gorgeous, bubbly cheerleader and the completely natural, conservative person she had become? A smile relaxed her face for the first time in hours. She'd always wanted to be a fly on the wall at Jefferson High School; maybe tonight would be her chance. And to think she had been seriously considering ditching her ten-year reunion to stay home and read a good book. She wouldn't miss this party for the world!

* * *

She drove her 1985 faded green El Camino into the parking lot of the Landry Hotel. Oh great! Valet parking. As if she had money for a tip tonight after splurging on clothes. Megan sighed in exasperation as she handed her keys over to the smirking attendant and noticed that his derision of her car didn't pass on to her legs. She squared her shoulders and walked into the lobby of the elegant hotel. There were enough marble pillars and faux Greek statues for a remake of Spartacus. *Why couldn't the reunion have been held in the old school gym?* she grumbled under her breath. *And why was she starting to feel like an old piece of chewed-up gum?* Megan's pace slowed as it dawned on her that everyone she saw was dressed in tuxedos and formals. Everyone except her.

She veered to the right instead of heading for the ballroom, where everyone else was going. Pausing behind an unnaturally large potted palm tree, she ripped the invitation from her purse. Where did it say the evening was formal?! She would look like a fool. Megan scanned the now-wrinkled paper, finally noticing the very small, neat black letters on the bottom left-hand side of the paper. Formal attire suggested.

She leaned back and closed her eyes, then banged her head in frustration against the wall. At least the oversized plant was shielding her from everyone. She would die if anyone she knew recognized her now. There was no way that she was going to humiliate herself tonight. She'd had enough humiliation to last a lifetime. No thank you.

Easing away from the wall, she tried to blend in with the shadows as she headed for the exit, pasting a serene and completely fake smile on her face and trying to act as if she had no idea there was a school reunion going on. Who had ever heard of Jefferson High School? Besides that, who had ever heard of Megan Garrett?

Megan was so busy looking calm, yet purposeful, she didn't even notice the man standing in the shadows on the opposite side of the foyer watching her. He could see that she was leaving and he wasn't about to let that happen. Taking the woman beside him by the hand, he glided smoothly over to intercept her.

"Well, if it isn't Megan Garrett," Dylan Carlisle drawled.

Megan stumbled back, aghast to see the man she had once believed herself to be in love with. He was still handsome, only more so now that he was older. He had been a pretty boy in high school; now he was just plain gorgeous. His blond hair was swept back, still thick and full, and his blue eyes looked silver. He really should have been a model. At least that's what he had always told her.

Megan glanced past his left shoulder and noticed a woman who was trying her best to go unnoticed. Turning slightly Megan looked into the nervous eyes of Taffie Barlow Carlisle. They had been co-captains of the cheerleading squad together and had been best friends. Keyword: had.

"You remember Megan, don't you, Taffie? She's the one who humiliated me in front of all my friends and family. To think I actually thought I loved her once! Taffie, hand me a piece of gum will you? I'm getting a bad taste in my mouth."

Megan blinked as Taffie dug into her evening bag, searching as if her life depended on it. Not three seconds passed before she placed the gum in Dylan's outstretched hand. He chewed the gum a few moments before he continued.

"I have to say I'm surprised you even showed up tonight. I didn't think you had the guts. But now that I see you standing here . . ." Dylan let his gaze fall to her PayLess clearance shoes, to her Wal-Mart skirt and blouse, and settled at last on her face. It was obvious she had come up lacking. He smiled slowly, which brought a malicious warmth to his eyes that hadn't been there before.

"Hmm. This might not be so bad after all. As a matter of fact, this is going to be perfect," he sneered.

Megan opened her mouth for the first time since coming face to face with her ex-boyfriend, and ex-fiance.

"Excuse me, but I left my cell phone in the car." Megan turned to flee but was stopped by Dylan's harsh laughter and tight grip on her arm.

"Forget about your phone, Megan. You're coming with us. I wouldn't be able to live with myself if you missed even a second of tonight's festivities."

Megan shook off his hand and glared up into the eyes of the man she had come so close to spending eternity with.

"I'm not going anywhere with you, Dylan. Not then, not now, not ever. Don't worry though, I'm not leaving. I wouldn't miss this reunion for anything, not even for you. And since I don't plan on mingling with you two tonight, I'll just leave you with one bit of advice if you want to have a good time. Stop living in the past and get over it."

As she preceded them into the ballroom, she decided she'd rather be cleaning toilets. In fact, seeing all the glittering, polished women, in their exquisite formals, she wished she could trade the whole evening in for a men's locker room of dirty toilets.

She forced herself to walk nonchalantly over to the table of name tags, but couldn't help an involuntary groan when she saw they all had pictures from their senior year attached. If the tags hadn't been laminated, she would have torn her picture off. She stuck her name tag up high on her shoulder, hoping that her hair would hide it, then scanned the ballroom for a possible escape. Noticing a fire exit on the opposite side, she moved swiftly around the groups of laughing, smiling people, she once knew and vowed that she would make it up to them at their twenty-year reunion.

"Hey, I noticed you when you walked in with Dylan and Taffie. I can't read your tag, but you look so familiar. What's your name?"

Megan knew it would be rude to keep walking. She was desperate, but she wasn't rude. She turned to answer the tall attractive woman who had waylaid her and squealed, grabbing the surprised woman in a bear hug, laughing in delight. "Brenna!"

"I must have a really bad memory, because I just can't place your name." The woman gasped out, after having all the air squeezed out of her lungs.

Megan grinned at the confusion and pulled the hair off of her name tag. "Let me help you out a little."

Brenna leaned in closer, squinting in the dim light. "Megan Garrett! No! It can't be you."

Brenna stared at her for the longest time, making Megan wish she had checked her teeth for lettuce. She couldn't be that different. She had wanted to go unnoticed tonight, but Brenna's apparent disbelief was a little disconcerting. Megan started to reach for her driver's license, when she was stopped by Brenna's arms gripping her shoulders.

"I had no idea you were so beautiful. I mean, you were always cute, but look at you now!"

Megan's mouth dropped. This woman was insane. It had been approximately two and a half years since anyone had paid her a compliment, and she hadn't believed the clerk at the gas station then either.

"Um, thanks. So how have you been Brenna? Did you get your medical degree so you can save the world?"

Brenna still looked stunned momentarily, then laughed.

"Well, no. I ended up getting married my third year in college. I had to drop out to support my husband, and four kids and a dog later, here I am."

But Megan could tell from the happy sparkle in Brenna's eyes that she didn't regret her choice at all. She glanced at her own bare left hand, regretting that she had never found anyone that could make her eyes sparkle like her old friend's.

"Megan, what happened to you? I mean, you've changed so much. Are you married, divorced, widowed? Are you working? Where do you live? And how do you stay a size six?"

Megan laughed, remembering the fun conversations they'd had as chemistry partners. She would have flunked chemistry flat out if it hadn't been for Brenna Colburn. And Brenna had made it so fun for, that Megan had even looked forward to fifth period. It was too bad they hadn't stayed close. There had been many times in her life since graduation when Megan had needed a good friend.

"Okay, I'm not married and never have been. I'm a real estate agent now. I live in Lehi. And my rotten, evil pest of a dog eats all my food."

Brenna laughed, hugging Megan happily.

"That's what I always liked about you. You were always so literal."

Megan smiled back at Brenna, noticing the changes in her friend as well. Whereas Megan had stopped bleaching her hair, Brenna had added red highlights to her dark brown hair. And while she wasn't a size six, she had filled out very attractively. She looked wonderful. And she wasn't wearing a formal either! She was wearing a very classy suit. What a relief!

"So where's your husband? I'd like to meet the man who could take on the brain of the century."

Brenna snorted, nodding over to the buffet table.

"They're serving shrimp—where else would he be? He's addicted to seafood in the very worst way. But I do love him. Oh you know him! Don't you remember Jack Harrison? No? Well I remember he used to have the most enormous crush on you! It used to make me so mad, since I always knew I was going to marry him someday, and you didn't even know he existed."

Jack Harrison? Megan had absolutely no clue, so she just nodded her head and smiled.

Brenna's mouth quirked up on one side. She had always been able to read Megan like a book. Everyone else had only seen what Megan had wanted them to see, but Brenna had always enjoyed looking deeper, and had been rewarded for it by discovering a very kind, genuine person.

"Now, correct me if I'm wrong, but weren't you supposed to marry Dylan Carlisle? I think I even got a wedding invitation in the mail. I would have come, but I had just accepted a job as a nanny for the summer in New York. So what happened?"

Megan cleared her throat uncomfortably, glancing around the ballroom, wishing desperately for an interruption. Nothing.

"We didn't get married."

Brenna frowned at Megan and raised an eyebrow.

"Yeah."

Megan's shoulders relaxed and she laughed. She really laughed.

"Oh Brenna. Take me to lunch some time and I promise to spill my guts for you."

"I'm already planning on it. You'll have to settle for McDonald's though."

Brenna grabbed her planner out of her purse and wrote down Megan's phone number and address. They only lived twenty miles away from each other.

As Brenna made her way back to her husband, Megan smiled and turned away to continue her escape. Dress and

Dylan aside, running into Brenna had made tonight worth it.

Megan scanned the crowd for any more potential delays or obstacles, and then once again headed for the exit. She didn't feel the overwhelming urge to start screaming and running at the same time, but she still felt very uncomfortable. She should have assumed Dylan would be here, or at the very least she should have come up with a date. Not that she was having the best of luck in that area lately. It had been three and a half months since her last date, and there wasn't any sign of that pattern changing anytime soon.

An unexpected hand on her arm made her jump, as tense as she was. Embarrassed, she nevertheless forced herself to relax and smile as she turned toward the next classmate to seek her attention and felt her cheeks burn. Dylan again. She wasn't even surprised.

"Ah, Megan! Sorry about that. I didn't mean to scare you. Feeling a little nervous tonight perhaps? Afraid no one will recognize you? You remember all of our old crowd, don't you? Let's see if they remember you."

Dylan laughed as he pulled her toward a group of people standing nearby. This was almost more than she could stand. It had been over for years now. He was married. Was he still active in the church? Or had her rejection of him at the last moment caused him to fall away entirely from his beliefs? Their beliefs?

"Hi, Mark. Hi, Kurt. Connor, Dan, Nick." She did her best to smile at the men and their wives.

Mark, who had always been kind to her in school, reached out his hand and shook hers politely.

"Hi, Megan. It's good to see you again. This is my wife, Cleo."

Megan felt her hands begin to shake and knew she was very close to crying. She had to leave quickly, but with Dylan's hand still on her arm, she was imprisoned.

Thinking quickly, she stomped on Dylan's foot as hard as her high heels would allow, and smiled in relief as he let go of her arm quickly

"It was nice to see all of you guys again," she said. "Enjoy the rest of the evening."

She turned blindly and headed in the opposite direction from Dylan. She had to get away from him. She wasn't quick enough to out-distance his voice though.

"Hey, Megan, where's your date tonight? Or did you stand him up, too?"

Megan stopped in her tracks, stunned by Dylan's rudeness. She turned to stare at Dylan, her mouth gaping open. How could anyone be so cruel? The crowd of ex-cronies dispersed quite suddenly from around Dylan, leaving him gloating. It was clear he was enjoying himself. He evidently wanted to humiliate Megan in front of an audience, and he was doing a fine job of it. Taffie gave her an apologetic glance before grabbing her husband's arm and pulling him away. Megan stood by herself, stunned by the verbal attack. She couldn't move. If she did, she would break into a thousand pieces.

"Excuse me," said an unfamiliar, though not unpleasant voice.

Megan closed her mouth slowly. Who in the world would want to talk to her after witnessing such a scene? She looked around.

"Yes?"

He was a little over six foot, lean but not wimpy, with broad shoulders. His hair was either dark brown or black, and his eyes were dark, too. He looked furious, as if he wanted to hit someone. Megan thought he seemed hard, as if life was aging him faster than it should. But then he smiled at her, cracking the severeness of his face, and putting her at ease. He was actually very striking, once you got past the scary part.

"I was wondering if you would like something to drink? You

look like you could use one about now."

Megan took the glass he held out to her gratefully. She downed the liquid quickly, and looked up to see the stranger's sympathetic gaze still on her.

"I'm sorry, but I couldn't help overhearing what just happened. I'm a little confused. Did I hear Dylan Carlisle say you were Megan Garrett?"

Megan looked at the stranger more carefully. Did she know this man? She must if he was here for the reunion.

"Among other things."

The man's kind eyes looked her over more carefully, shaking his head in confusion. She felt like a scientific experiment gone wrong.

"Thanks for the drink. Good-bye."

Megan shoved the glass back into the man's hands and attempted to walk away, when he reached out and grabbed her hand, pulling her back to face him. He quickly placed the glass on the floor beside him and put two fingers in his mouth, whistling as loudly as a train, successfully getting everyone's attention in the room. Megan wasn't sure what was going on, but life was starting to get too weird. She instantly took back all her kind thoughts about the man. He was definitely a convict.

Then he moved in closer and took her face in his hands, leaning down as if he was intent on getting something out of her eye. His smooth, firm lips came as a complete surprise to her. She pushed at his shoulders with all the strength she had, but he was a brick wall. The man didn't seem in a big hurry to end the kiss either. Not that it was a bad kiss, but something had to be done. Megan brought her knee up as swiftly and as accurately as she could, but was blocked by his quick move to the side. He had been anticipating her. She had missed her target, but had been successful in ending the kiss.

"If you ever touch me again, so help me I'll . . ." Megan panted as she tried to catch her breath and finish her threat.

The man grinned crookedly down at her and then cleared his throat theatrically.

"She may have a reputation for standing men up, but with a kiss like that, I'd say she's worth the risk!" His voice carried quite well in the large room.

Hearing the laughter and cat calls that surrounded her, Megan took a deep calming breath and then slapped him as hard as she could. Then she turned on her heels and practically ran for the exit. What did she need her dignity for now? She was getting out of here if she had to fight her way out. She was mere seconds from freedom when she heard the announcement.

"Attention ladies and gentlemen. We're going to go ahead and begin. Don't worry, the buffet will be open all night. We're going to hand out a few awards now, but the kicker is, at the end of the awards ceremony, we're going to auction off the winners! If you ever wanted to dance with the prom queen or king, here's your chance. All the proceeds will go to help buy new textbooks for Jefferson High School."

Megan paused in her flight at the door. All she had to do was walk through it, and she was free. But an invisible chain had wrapped itself around her ankles. She reminded herself that she hadn't mingled with everyone as she had originally planned to, and she was still curious as to how everyone had changed. Who had become successful, and who had gained twenty pounds. It couldn't hurt if she just stood here in the doorway and watched. She was safe now. No one would notice her here. Dylan and the insane stranger weren't in sight. Maybe she could stick around for a few more minutes.

"We've had our spies out and about tonight, getting all the goods on everybody, so don't be surprised if we call out your name. Along with your award tonight, you'll receive a gift certificate for two for dinner at The Roof! And for those people who proved us right, they get a free carriage ride around

Temple Square. So let's get started; we want to have plenty of time for dancing later. All right then, does everyone remember who was voted most likely to get plastic surgery?"

Megan giggled along with everyone else, and felt bad for Taffie when her high school picture was plastered on a tall screen in front of everybody.

"According to our sources, Taffie did have a little augmentation work done, but you'll have to ask her where. Come on up, Gorgeous, and get in line for the auction!"

Megan felt her own cheeks turn red on Taffie's behalf, but was surprised when Taffie strutted up to the stage grinning and winking at everyone. She was loving the attention. It reminded Megan of when they were cheerleaders. Back then Megan herself wouldn't have been fazed by the attention, but now strutting anywhere, least of all on stage, was the last thing she wanted to do.

"Next, who remembers the most likely to end up in jail? No one? Troy Stafford!"

Troy's picture was plastered on the wall, and even though he did look a little rough in his high school picture, she remembered Troy as being one of the few sincerely kind people in high school. Megan searched the crowd looking for Troy.

"Ah, hah! There you are, Troy!"

The spotlight hit Troy right in the face, as he was trying to look invisible. *Poor guy,* Megan sympathized.

"Our sources tell us that we were dead wrong on that one. Troy not only did not end up in jail, he has never even had a speeding ticket. He teaches special education classes at Addison Junior High. He's been married for six years and has three children. Let's all give Troy a hand for proving us wrong."

Troy had turned practically purple in mortification. Megan wondered if they were going to be tasteless and actually announce the classmate who had ended up in jail. Indeed they were.

"Jared Runion," the announcer called out. "You win the prize for jail time. We won't say what for—we'll let everyone keep guessing. But it's your lucky night, buddy, because you just won yourself and a date, dinner at The Roof! I'd take my parole officer if I were you."

Jared sauntered uncaringly up to the stage, seemingly untouched by the public knowledge of his downfall. Amazing. Megan hadn't known Jared all that well in school. All she could remember about him was that he had always been extremely worried about grades and deadlines. It most likely had something to do with taxes.

"This next one is good. The most likely to succeed. Who can forget Dylan Carlisle? Running back for the football team and class president. Hmm. According to our sources, Dylan has done very well for himself working in his father's advertising firm; however, we feel the most successful member of our class would have to be Trevor Riley. Trevor was president of his seminary class and a member of the karate club. Why don't you head on down to the stage while I make everyone jealous of you, Trevor."

Megan watched Dylan's spot-lighted face as it became a mask of diffidence. She knew he was furious behind his bland smile.

"Trevor started his own company eight years ago, after his mission to Guatemala. He is now worth—now I'm not making this up guys—eleven million dollars. We got that little tidbit of information from Forbes magazine, by the way. So I hope all you single women will start counting your money for the auction, because as of now, he's still unattached, too."

Megan tore her gaze away from Dylan and glanced up on stage to see the man who had defended her so audaciously just minutes before. Who was he? Megan racked her brain for any memory at all of this guy and still came up blank. Had she been that oblivious to the people around her in high school? He was very interesting to look at; she was sure she wouldn't have forgotten a face like his. She turned her eyes towards his year-book picture emblazoned on the wall, and felt all of the forgotten memories resurface. Trevor. Of course, the seminary president. But he had been off limits. She could still remember the crush she'd had on him so long ago. They had both been so different back then.

He had been in a completely different social circle than hers. He had been attractive back then, but there was a different quality about him now. She didn't remember him being so tall either. She recalled how she used to catch him staring at her in the hallways and cafeteria. She couldn't help returning the favor now.

Megan let the announcer's voice drone on and on as she stood there like a mannequin and stared at Trevor. He looked very uncomfortable by all of the attention. Why hadn't he ever gotten married? What was his story? If he was as rich as they said, she wouldn't mind selling him a house, that was for sure. She'd take a commission from anyone these days. Even someone like him.

When she heard the category for the most popular girl and boy, she knew that was her cue to leave. She had been voted most popular her senior year; she still had the CD player her father had given her as a reward. She hadn't meant to stay so long, but now it was too late. As the spotlight blinded her, she closed her eyes and tried not to listen to the announcer's words. And to think she could have been halfway home by now.

"According to our sources, Megan isn't the party girl she used to be. She sells real estate for Western Realty, she's still single, but she does have a dog, ladies and gentlemen, so don't feel too bad for her. At least it's not a cat.

"And now the moment you've been waiting for. The most popular girl now, would have to be . . . Brooke Truman! Brooke works as a flight attendant for Delta Airlines, and assures us that she does indeed have a boyfriend in every port. Come on down, Brooke, and stand by the winners."

As everyone's attention switched to the stage, Megan felt herself relax. No one was staring at her anymore, no one cared what she did for a living or if she did stay home every night. She smiled. She had lost the contest and she couldn't be more relieved. At least they hadn't asked her to walk up on the stage in front of everyone. Now that would have killed her.

"Now this last category is one we just made up at the last minute, but I think you'll agree with us, when you hear what it is. The most unrecognizable classmate. Now there was no way we could vote on this ten years ago, but we'll throw in the carriage ride anyway if Megan Garrett wouldn't mind taking a walk down memory lane. Come on down, sweetheart, and let us all have a better look at you."

Megan felt her skin turn to ice and her eyelids freeze to her eyeballs. She forced herself to move her uncooperative limbs as she stumbled towards the lobby. What a fool she had been! Even after she'd been spotlighted, she had stayed, lurking in the doorway. That was it. Her parents were right. She was crazy.

"There she goes, boys! After her!"

Megan began a full-on sprint after hearing the announcer's words. What was this, a fox hunt?! Could she sue for public humiliation? Megan threw her keys at the valet attendant and ran outside to stand behind a pillar. Thirty long seconds passed. Come on! How hard could it be to find an El Camino amongst all of the Ford Expeditions and Lincoln Navigators? The cool wind of the night soothed her red cheeks as she stood there, with her hands clenched at her side. Why anyone ever showed up at reunions was beyond her.

"Megan, please come back inside. It will be worse if you don't. You have to face down your enemy. Running only drags it out. Trust me."

Megan peeked from behind the pillar where she was hiding. It was Brenna. Brenna?

"Don't make me do this, Brenna," Megan pleaded. "I can't handle this right now. You didn't hear how Dylan embarrassed me in front of all of those people in there. And then Trevor—can you believe he kissed me? I really don't enjoy crying in front of crowds, so if you'll just tell the valet to hurry for me, I will be eternally grateful."

Brenna walked slowly around the pillar, as if she were cornering a wild animal, and held out her hand.

"Dylan has a bet going around for five hundred dollars that you'll chicken out. I'm almost positive he's the one who put the reunion committee up to the extra category. Let's go back inside, Megan. Just think about how small Dylan is going to feel when he has to ask Daddy for a loan to cover all of his bets. I made Jack bet against him, and Jack doesn't bet. Come on, we're using our kids' college funds."

Megan felt the blood swimming in her veins, and the steel returning to her spine. Dylan was betting on her, as if she were a dog at the races. Fine, she wouldn't mind ruining his night and his bank account, even if she did feel like the main attraction in a freak show.

"Okay. Let's go."

Brenna put her arm protectively around Megan's shoulders as she escorted her through the now quiet groups of people and to the steps leading onto the stage.

Just thinking of Brenna's kids working at Taco Bell to support themselves through school had Megan forcing a smile onto her stiff face. She repeated the words, "This too shall pass" over and over in her mind as a mantra, while she was being escorted to the line of "winners."

"Thank you Brenna for tracking Megan down for us. It usually helps to have the after picture to go along with the before. It's not very fun otherwise. All right, now who out there recognized our own little Megan when she walked in the door tonight? Now be honest! Anyone? No? I didn't think so."

Megan moved her eyes over the crowd, relieved that Dylan

had kept his hand down. He had recognized her immediately. Why was that? Megan turned her head a fraction and noticed they hadn't been satisfied with her yearbook picture and had picked a shot of her doing a back flip off a pyramid of other cheerleaders. She actually liked the shot, except for the fact that her behind took up most of the picture. Megan blinked back the tears that threatened to fall. Why hadn't she just promised to send Brenna's kids a check in the mail, postdated fifteen years?

Standing beside her, Trevor whispered, "Don't let them get to you. Just picture yourself at The Roof, stuffing your face with grilled salmon and creme brulee, while everyone else is eating leftover Tuna Helper."

Megan frowned suspiciously at Trevor. How did he know that was what she'd had last night for dinner? And why was he being so nice to her? Megan winced as she looked at his face, the cheek she had slapped was still noticeably reddened. The kiss really hadn't been that bad. She almost regretted slapping him. But not quite.

"All right, folks. It's the time you've all been waiting for. Let's all get our checkbooks out, because it's time to spend some money! I personally know of a couple guys right off the top of my head, that would have killed to dance with Taffie in high school. Myself included. Wives and girlfriends, just turn your heads and think of all the nice new textbooks the kids will be getting. Here's your chance, boys. Who will start me off with one hundred dollars?"

Megan wasn't surprised Taffie went for a thousand dollars. On the other hand, she would be very surprised if she went for more than twenty-five cents. The announcer went through the line quickly, selling off Trevor for a measly fifty bucks.

"Now, last of all, our captain of the cheerleaders. Is there anyone out there who has waited ten years to dance with Megan Garrett? Dylan's not around to fight everyone off this time. Who will start me off with one hundred dollars? All right, all right. Fifty?"

Megan closed her eyes in agony as the ballroom became completely quiet. If she wrote a check for herself, would they let her go home?

"I'll give you five thousand dollars for a dance with Megan."

Megan choked as her eyes shot open. What idiot . . . ? Trevor? The announcer looked taken aback, but was obviously pleased by the amount bid. Who wouldn't be?

"Trust me, I would love to accept your bid, but you're already taken. Our own Ms. Wilburn, who by the way still teaches art at Jefferson High School, has already given us a check for your time."

Trevor turned to catch Megan's eye and winked at her. Megan was too shocked to do anything but stare back stupidly.

"If it's all the same to you, I would actually prefer to collect my dance at a later time. I wouldn't miss dancing with Ms. Wilburn for anything."

Applause filled the ballroom, and Megan found her mouth twitching at the charming way Trevor had handled the problem. She was free. She wanted to thank Trevor for bidding on her, but he had already been claimed by Ms. Wilburn. Since there was really nothing keeping her at the reunion, she collected her gift certificate and did what she had been aching all night to do. She left.

Chapter 2

Trevor was stunned. He had assumed she would wait for him. He shook his head as the valet went to get his rental car. She had taken off just like Cinderella, and hadn't even had the courtesy to leave him a shoe. Or her phone number, for that matter. He leaned up against a pillar and pictured her in his mind again. Megan. Wow. He could hardly believe it was her. She had transformed herself from every teenage boy's wildest dream into a sophisticated man's vision of a perfect woman. Who'd have ever guessed that under all the hairspray, blond curls, blue contact lenses and risqué clothes, she was a classic beauty? That's the word that fit her now. Classy. Trevor smiled. She was just what he had been looking for.

His thoughts were interrupted by a voice that sounded as frustrated as he felt. "What is the matter with you? The party has just started, and there'll be dancing for another few hours. Let go of me! I don't want to go home, Dylan."

Trevor moved back towards the wall, so he wouldn't be noticed. This could be interesting.

"She ruined it. She ruined everything. I can't go back in there. Besides, all those guys are going to want their money. Do you want to be the one to tell them we're broke? You've spent every last dime we had. There's no way I can pay off everyone. Uh uh. We're long gone."

Trevor leaned forward and saw Taffie with her arms folded across her chest and a fighting look in her eyes. He smiled, anticipating what she would say to her husband.

"Well, I'm not going home. I'm staying, and if anyone comes up to me looking for you, I'll be as nice as can be and give them your cell number. I told you to leave her alone, but you can't, can you? It's pathetic how obsessed you are even after eight years. She made her choice, Dylan. It wasn't you. It will never be you. I'm your wife. If you spent half as much time thinking about me, as you do her, I'd be in heaven. Don't worry about how I'll get home. I'll find a ride."

With that, she flipped her long blond hair over her shoulder and walked quickly back to the ballroom. Ouch! Trevor eased away from the wall, just enough to be seen. It seemed as if the pot was getting ready to boil, and he didn't mind sticking his spoon in for a little stir.

"Great party, huh?" he drawled, giving Dylan a lazy smile.

Dylan flinched noticeably, turning to glare at Trevor.

"Is that how you made your millions, eavesdropping? A little insider trading? You always were a sneaky son-of-a . . ."

Trevor's eyebrows raised slightly. He would freely admit he had been eavesdropping, but he would never have described himself as "sneaky." He decided to ignore that little jab and dish out one of his own.

"Didn't Megan look beautiful tonight, Dylan? I was just about knocked off my feet. And what a kisser! Why anyone would let someone like her get away is beyond me. What on earth were you thinking, Dylan?"

Dylan sneered at Trevor and turned to walk away, but suddenly found himself face to face with Trevor.

"If you ever harass Megan again, you'll regret it. Do you understand me?"

Dylan's eyes narrowed and he took a step backwards as he threw a hard right at Trevor. Moving back and automatically blocking the first swing, Trevor ducked the second and went into a defensive position, waiting. Dylan stood, breathing hard with his fists clenched, not sure what to do next. Trevor nodded his head to something, or someone behind Dylan.

"Dylan, I think your friends are looking for you."

Dylan turned to see who Trevor was talking about and saw a group of unsmiling men he had made the ill-fated bet with.

"Don't forget what I just said about Megan. I'm going to be watching out for her now. Remember that."

Trevor turned and took his keys from the shocked young valet, who wasn't too shocked not to smile at the tip.

Driving away from the hotel, Trevor headed up the canyon to a secluded and private cabin he was borrowing from a friend. He thought about what had happened at his ten-year reunion and laughed. He laughed so hard he had to pull over to the side of the road until he regained control. Here he was, acting like a complete teenager. A macho one at that. If his mother had seen him, she would have dragged him out of the hotel by his ear. He had always had the urge to protect Megan and he had finally gotten his chance. Trevor laughed again, as he realized he was acting out his teenage fantasies. Man, he needed therapy. It would serve him right, if Megan was hiding a very large, very possessive boyfriend somewhere. Trevor reached for his phone and punched a button that automatically dialed his private secretary.

"Blaine? . . . Yeah, it was great. Hey listen, take this down. Megan Garrett. She lives somewhere in Utah County, I think. Find out everything you can on her. Have it to me by tomorrow morning. Got it? Thanks."

Trevor hit the gas, continuing on his way. He couldn't stop smiling. He was always happiest when he was on the brink of a new project. Megan Garrett didn't realize it, but she had just become Trevor Riley's next project.

Chapter 3

Megan looked out the garden window in her kitchen, and felt so calm and peaceful that she never wanted to leave the house again. Bad things happened when you did. Megan shook her head and smiled at the thought, then gasped as her border collie attacked her weeping cherry tree. Ergh! Megan tried hard not to think some very uncharitable thoughts about her dog, Marjorie. So instead of daydreaming of taking her dog to the pound, she grabbed her scriptures and headed out the door. It was fast Sunday and she didn't want to be late. Hearing everyone's testimonies was her favorite part of church. Not that she'd ever had the guts to get up and bear hers, but she knew someday she would. Just not yet.

Megan turned to lock her front door, and paused to look up at her one and only extravagance. She had driven by the house one day, seen the "For Sale" sign, and had fallen immediately in love. Being thirty thousand dollars below appraisal hadn't hurt either. Yes, it had needed a few repairs. Like a million. But the simple charm of the old house had caught her imagination. Growing up, Megan had either lived with her parents or with roommates in cramped apartments, but this was her home. The red brick, dormer windows, chimney, and half-acre lot had seemed to call out to her. And she had answered back, using all of the money in her savings for a down payment. Dylan had been furious with her at the time, wasting her money on a house that he refused to live in. He had been set on an exclusive condo close to school so he could finish up his degree. It was the one thing she refused to budge on.

But even with a huge down payment, she still had a

monster of a mortgage. She'd thought at the time she could easily handle it considering the substantial salary she had been earning at Royden, Powell, and Associates as executive secretary working for Dylan's uncle. Sadly, she was laid off from that fine establishment right after she dumped Dylan (surprise, surprise). She had since found that her love for houses had translated nicely into joining the real estate game.

Reality had been sinking in one mortgage payment at a time, and now she knew for sure she couldn't handle it, unless she actually started selling houses, of course. She'd only sold two during the past six months, and was still living off the last of her commission, which unfortunately, didn't leave very much left over for food.

Thinking of food had her wondering what in the world she was going to make for lunch. She had a choice between macaroni and cheese and Marjorie's kibble. Boy, was she looking forward to using the gift certificate to The Roof. At the moment, thoughts of salmon and creme brulee were powerful enough to push the embarrassing memories of last night back into a corner. She found herself smiling as she walked to church.

* * *

Three and a half hours later, as she sat alone at her small kitchen table and poked at her soggy macaroni, she didn't feel like smiling anymore. She did have her limits. She reached for the phone. Maybe if her mother was in a good mood, she would invite Megan over for Sunday dinner. The thought of pot roast with potatoes and carrots had her mouth watering as she dialed the number quickly. She'd ignore whatever rude comments they wanted to say to her, as long as she could have second helpings.

"Hello?"

"Hi, Mom. It's me, Megan. How are you guys doing? I haven't talked to you for a while."

"Oh, you know us dear. We're doing great. How's the real estate market lately? I hope it's picked up since last time we talked."

Megan blew the hair out of her eyes and wondered how to steer the conversation around to food.

"Hmmm. Well, Jackie sold a house last week, and Dean has an earnest money agreement written up. So yeah, I think things are looking good for us."

"You didn't mention yourself, dear. Have you sold anything lately?"

Megan pursed her lips in frustration. She did have the tendency to come away from conversations with her parents slightly depressed. Was the food really worth it? At the moment, she wasn't sure.

"Not yet, but I have high hopes for one family. They've come in twice, and I think I have them narrowed down to a wonderful home in American Fork. They have the cutest little girl; I just want to steal her and take her home with me."

"You could have had a cute little girl of your own by now, if things had been different. But it's no use crying over spilt milk, right? Well dear, I've got to be going. It's been nice chatting with you, but your father is taking me and your sister out to lunch at Mulboon's. You know how we all love those shrimp bowls. I'd invite you of course, but since you've become so zealous about religion, I wouldn't want to offend you."

Megan got up and placed her bowl of macaroni and cheese in the microwave after saying good-bye to her mother, and tried to no avail to think of anything besides large bowls of fresh shrimp and tangy cocktail sauce.

She really shouldn't complain. She had actually been invited over for Sunday dinner by Drew Jarvis, a kind man in his mid-forties and a widower. He was actually handsome, too, in an English sort of way, if you could get past the fact that he was still very much in love with his wife, who had died two years ago from breast cancer. He taught American Heritage at the community college to support five very active children. He had been asking her to come for dinner for the last month and a half and she hadn't accepted even one of his invitations, mostly because she didn't want to lead him on. Plus, she had the distinct impression that he was on the lookout for a new babysitter/housekeeper/wife. She couldn't even handle one rotten dog—how could she handle five kids? But wouldn't it show her mother?!

Megan continued to pick woefully at her inadequate dinner as she eyed the bag of dog food she had just purchased at PetSmart. Maybe if she added enough gravy, it might taste like a roast? She shook her head as she swallowed another bite, before laying down her fork.

Megan paused as she reached for the keys, wondering what kind of food they served in homeless shelters. With her luck, it would be macaroni and cheese. Going out to the backyard, she walked over to her dog and patted her head a couple of times. She glanced at her now-battered cherry tree and growled at the dog, which only incited further excited barking. No one took her seriously, not even her dog, Megan sighed.

Megan pulled out of her driveway and headed to her usual spot. The parking lot beside the Mount Timpanogos Temple in American Fork. Second only to her house, it was her favorite place to be. She tried going to the temple at least once a week, but Sundays, when she was usually all alone, was when she needed the peace and sense of beauty the most. She turned the motor off and tilted the seat back as far as it would go before resting her head on her hands and gazing up at the stained glass. She liked to use her time in front of the temple to think and pray and go over her goals in life. She had started this ritual of parking in front of temples when she had been a freshman in college, and it had helped her get through some very difficult situations. As she closed her eyes and felt the sun caress her face, she smiled once again. She would never trade her life now for what it had been. Macaroni, dog, and all.

Chapter 4

Trevor took one last bite of the chicken enchiladas with green chili sauce his mom had made especially for him and laid his fork down, despite the frown he received.

"Mom, after three helpings, even I get stuffed. I loved them. Who wouldn't? Can I take some back to the cabin with me? I promise to eat some more before I go to bed later. I promise!"

Cora Riley glared at her son's plate and then smiled suddenly, making him instantly suspicious.

"I wouldn't have to stuff you so much if I had a daughter-in-law and say, three grandkids to spoil. It would really make things easier on you. And I know the perfect girl. Short black hair, great blue eyes, and dimples to die for. Hmm? What do you think? I'm good friends with her mother. We bowl every Tuesday morning together. I could set the two of you up tomorrow. You're in town for how long? A week? Two? You could be engaged in a few weeks . . . ."

Trevor pushed back from the table and grinned at his mother as she rambled on, spinning her dreams for him. He should have moved back years ago. His mother needed family around her, and all of the times he had flown her up to Washington didn't really cut it. She had two sisters and a brother who lived nearby with their children, but that was different. Trevor was her only child, since his dad had died in Vietnam before he was even born. His mother had never remarried, although she was a petite, attractive woman. Cora had spent all of her time working to support the two of them. She had taken jobs cleaning houses wherever she could find the work, and she had made enough to support the two of them, send him on a mission, and put him through college. She was incredible.

It was time for paybacks. Although she had refused all of the vacations he had wanted to send her on, she did accept jewelry. It had taken three years and countless arguments to get her to stop cleaning houses and retire. He had finally convinced her that being a volunteer was much more fulfilling. Now it was time for more. He wanted to see her in a brand new home, somewhere safe and beautiful. But convincing her to move was almost impossible. But this way, he was killing two birds with one stone. Bribery could be so useful.

"Hold it, hold it! I'm way ahead of you, Mom."

Cora closed her mouth slowly, eyed her son, and searched for the teasing light in his eye. He looked dead serious. At thirty, maybe he was ready to settle. . . . Maybe she would have grandkids after all! Cora's face lit up as if a sun had burst inside her. With tears gleaming in her eyes, she rushed over to her son's side and cradled his head in her arms.

"Oh, you don't know how long I've been needing to hear the pitter-patter of little feet running around my house. And how long has it been since I've had a little sticky handprint on my window? They'll have dark hair and eyes like you, I bet. You have strong genes, Trev, just like your dad. Oh, you've made me so happy, I'm going to make you your favorite dessert! Coconut cream pie!"

Trevor felt a little hitch in his heart as he watched his mother float around her small, immaculate kitchen, dreaming of grandchildren. He shouldn't have waited so long.

"There are a couple of conditions you might want to consider before you start making that pie."

Cora turned slowly around and stared at her son with a steely gaze.

"What conditions?"

"You might want to sit down for this. I already have the

contract written up, and I have it right here with me. If you agree to the terms, then I will do all in my power to make your dreams of sticky fingers come true."

Cora stomped over to the table with a frown on her face and her hands on her hips.

"You know, you're too much like your father! Who else would make his own mother sign a contract? Just one or two is all I'm asking for! If I wanted four or five, I could see the need for a contract. What kind of conditions?"

Cora sat down at the table, still glaring at her son, but took the contract quickly, scanning the pages as if she had been a lawyer all of her life.

"I have to sell my house? Forget it!"

Trevor picked up a stray olive off of his plate and threw it in the air. Although he opened his mouth, ready to catch it, the olive bounced off his nose and dropped onto his brand-new leather shoes.

"I have to use the services of Megan Garrett? I don't even know her. Dennis' son is working for Wardley. I'll use him. He'll cut us a deal on the commission. I'll see to it."

Trevor shook his head and continued throwing olives in the air and missing them. Cora sniffed, and returned to the contract.

"I have to be as kind and as motherly to this Megan Garrett as humanly possible?! What is this?"

Cora dropped the contract as both hands went to her mouth. "She's the one. You want to marry this Megan Garrett! I see! Oh, of course I'll be nice to her. Why did you have to put that in the contract? You think I don't have good manners? You think I would be mean to the person who will bring my son so much happiness and give birth to my grandchildren? Shame on you!"

Trevor grinned at his mother but shook his head.

"You definitely have polite down pat, Mom, but when you

treat all the women who I introduce you to as if they were convicted felons hiding a secret wicked past, then yes, I do need to put that in the contract. For heaven's sake, when I introduced you to Alison, you made her cry!"

Trevor took one look at his mother's crestfallen face and quickly backpedaled.

"Hey, now don't get me wrong! That's one of the things I love about you. You're a mother bear and you always have been. You've been protecting me from bullies since I was two and now you've taken on suspicious females. All I'm saying is I want you to look closely at this woman. Look into her heart. Besides, it's a little difficult to get you those grandkids without a wife first. Not impossible, but very difficult."

Cora smoothed the pages of the contract out on the table, considering what her son was telling her. She had only wanted the best for her son. That wasn't a crime, but she could take it easy on Megan.

"That Alison was a golddigger, you mark my words. She was only after your money. Can I help it if I want someone to love my son for himself? Besides, that girl was so twitchy. Very guilty-looking. I could never trust a daughter-in-law with a twitchy eye."

Trevor choked on an olive as he sputtered and laughed.

"Mom, her contacts had sand in them. We had spent all day at the beach, and it had been windy that day. I can't believe this. You hexed a perfectly good relationship over a twitchy eye. And all she could talk about after that night was how much her other boyfriends' mothers had loved her, and why did my mom hate her so much. You're something else!"

Cora had the grace to blush, and decided that a change of subject would be in the best interest of everyone.

"I just don't understand why I have to sell my perfectly fine house just to meet this girl. And why make me look at, and I quote, 'lots with a view and having at least one-third of an acre in property.' And it says here that I have to inspect at least four lots. What if I find the perfect lot on the first try?"

Trevor got up from the table to get himself a glass of water from the sink and wished that his mother was one of those agreeable sorts who went along with everything their beloved sons wanted. But that just wasn't Cora Riley's style.

"Let's think grandkids here, Mom. You need at least a third of an acre for the swimming pool I'm going to put in. Kids love to swim on hot summer days. I know I did when I was kid."

Cora smiled at the image of children jumping and splashing in her own backyard.

"You know, a swing set wouldn't hurt either," Cora added softly, her eyes glowing.

Trevor smiled at his mom, knowing that all he had to do from now on was bring everything back to the welfare of her future grandchildren, and she was playdough in his hands.

"But why the stipulation of four lots? That seems a little odd to include in the contract."

Trevor sighed, knowing this one had nothing to do with curly-headed little moppets.

"I just thought it would be a good idea for you to spend some time with Megan. One on one, so that you two could get to know each other without me being in the equation. You see, I'm sort of planning on you to get the ball rolling for me. I want you to be the one to set me up on a date with her."

Cora rose from the table, kissed her son on the top of his head, patted his shoulder, and proceeded to get the ingredients out of the fridge for a coconut cream pie. Trevor stared at the unsigned contract lying ignored on the table, and at his surprisingly gleeful mother as she literally bounced around the kitchen. What was she up to?

Trevor cleared his throat politely to get his mother's attention.

"Um, Mom? I think you forgot one small detail here. You

have to actually sign the contract before we begin this little project."

Cora turned and smiled condescendingly at her son.

"My dear, I'm not signing anything until I actually meet Megan. Regardless of a new house and grandkids, my first priority is you and your happiness. Don't worry, though. I'll check her out first thing tomorrow. Don't worry sweetie! Everything's going to work out just fine, I promise!"

Trevor had mixed feelings as he watched his mother blithely gathering ingredients for her pie. He couldn't remember exactly why he had decided to include his mother. To think his future happiness depended on the woman who had ruined his last relationship because of a grain of sand.

He couldn't hold back the smile creeping out on his face, though, as he watched his mom work in the kitchen. Her mind was obviously far, far away on swimming and swinging grand-babies. She had just poured a cup of salt into what was supposed to be the pie crust. But he had made his mom happy, and that was worth something. It was worth a whole lot.

Chapter 5

Megan walked into the office of Western Realty with her shoulders squared and her head up. She was going to sell a house today. She was. Or it would be kibble for dinner.

"Hey, Megan! How was the big reunion?"

Megan tossed her purse and briefcase down behind her desk and smiled at Jackie Wilson, one of the other agents. Jackie's million-dollar smile had sold millions of dollars worth of houses, and she deserved every penny of her commissions. She was worth it. And she was nice. Even though they never saw each other outside of the office, Megan liked her very much. Jackie had bright, long red hair, beautiful blue eyes, and thousands of dollars worth of dental work, all of which contributed to a very active social life. She looked like a million bucks.

"You wouldn't believe me if I told you how horrible it was."

Jackie chuckled as she looked over a contract she was planning on signing later that day.

"I went to mine two years ago. I was the only one there who was divorced, and I hadn't brought a date. For some reason I had assumed I'd be dancing with all of my 'still single' ex-boyfriends. Boy, was I wrong. I sat in a corner the whole night and stuffed myself from the buffet. It was a nightmare. I think I gained three pounds."

Megan smiled sympathetically, berating herself for not stuffing her purse from the buffet before leaving. She hadn't been thinking clearly.

"Well, I don't think I'll be going back for my twenty-year reunion. Of course maybe by then they'll have lost the picture of my rear end they had plastered on the wall."

Jackie snorted, trying hard not to laugh outright.

"You're kidding me! If they had done that to me, my dad would have taken a horsewhip to whoever's bright idea that had been."

Megan's smile dimmed a little as she remembered she had no one to stick up for her. She was relieved when the phone rang and it was one of Jackie's clients. She didn't really want to relive every moment of that horrible, horrible night by sharing the details with her co-worker. She had to concentrate. She had to come up with a way to sell a house today. If she didn't, she'd have to go to her mom for money. The last time she had asked her mom for anything had been eight years ago after she'd been fired from Royden, Powell & Associates. She had been refused then and nothing had been offered since.

The bell over the door jingled, as a small, darkly attractive woman walked in. She looked to be in her late forties or early fifties. And she looked like business. Megan groaned, trying not to be jealous of Jackie's good fortune.

Megan looked over to get Jackie's nod and couldn't help it when her eyes widened in surprise. Jackie had written on a piece of notebook paper the words, "I'm swamped! Take her, please!" Megan shook her head suspiciously at Jackie. No real estate agent was ever too busy to take on a new client. Ever. Jackie smiled brightly and turned around in her swivel chair, showing Megan her back. Megan knew Jackie had to be aware of her lack of clients. She was just being very, very nice. Megan knew this was charity, but decided instantly that she would take it. When she was a million dollar producer like Jackie, she would pay her friend back.

Megan rose from her chair and quickly walked over to the woman who had picked up a brochure of homes for sale in the area.

"Hello. Can I help you?"

The lady put the brochure down and turned to stare at her. Megan cleared her throat nervously as the lady continued to stare without saying a word. Maybe she would just let Jackie have this one anyway, Megan thought.

"Are you Megan Garrett, or is the redhead Megan?"

Megan's eyebrows rose a fraction. Could this be a referral? The thought alone had her heart doing cartwheels. Word-of-mouth advertising was the only advertising she could afford at the moment. This must be her lucky day.

"I'm Megan."

The lady looked down and studied Megan's shoes, then worked her way up to the skirt she was wearing. The belt didn't take long, but when she came to the shirt, something kept her there for at least a minute, and then the woman moved up to Megan's face. The two women stared at each other, and Megan grew more and more alarmed. Why were people always staring at her? Either way, Megan's hopes for selling a house that day slowly dimmed and then completely disappeared. Now, how to get rid of the marathon starer?

"Was there something I could help you with today? Are you thinking of buying a new home, or selling?"

The woman, who was now staring hard at Megan's hair, ignored her completely. This was not going very well. Megan looked over her shoulder at Jackie. A rescue might become necessary. Jackie had another piece of notebook paper with "911?" written on it. Megan shook her head slightly. Hopefully she could handle this without calling in the big guns. Where was Stan, their broker, when she needed him?

"All right." The woman stated with a note of finality.

Megan's thoughts were stopped in midstride as the woman's simple statement brought her back. *All right?* That was it? Megan fidgeted slightly before answering.

"Umm, was that 'all right you wanted to buy a home,' or 'all right you wanted to sell a home?'"

The woman's stern face relaxed completely, and her eyes began to twinkle as she smiled at Megan. Megan looked back over her shoulder at Jackie again. This should teach her a lesson. Never accept charity walk-ins from other realtors. Of course this woman had known Megan's name, so she would have been stuck anyway.

"Would you like to look at some other brochures we have?" Megan asked slowly and clearly.

The woman opened her purse and popped a stick of gum into her mouth, before placing the sunglasses that had been resting on her head back over her eyes.

"I think you'll do nicely. Why don't we take a drive and I'll show you my house? I want you to sell it for me. A list of lots would be helpful too. I'm going to be building a new home. With a pool."

Megan tried to cover her mouth as she tried valiantly to keep from laughing. Something had just come over her, and she couldn't stop herself. She had never been hysterical before and wouldn't you know it would have to happen in front of a client who wanted her to sell her house for her? The woman looked very concerned for a moment, and then compassion filled her eyes. She walked over to Megan and patted her shoulder gently.

"Oh honey, it's okay. I've been there before too. Go on and grab your purse. I'll wait for you outside."

Megan went from hysterical laughter to unexplainable tears almost instantly. Both the commissions this woman was practically handing her on a silver platter were going to have to go for therapy. Hurrying to her desk, Megan grabbed her purse and briefcase, as well as her copy of the Multiple Listings book. Jackie was still on the phone, but gave her a thumbs-up signal encouragingly. Megan took a deep breath of air into her lungs, wiped the tears from her cheeks and ordered herself to be calm. She could do this. She didn't exactly have a choice.

The bright sunshine hit her right in the eyes as she tried to locate the woman. She wasn't standing beside the building—she was standing in the parking lot beside a brand new white Ford Excursion. It was monstrous-looking next to the petite woman, and completely incongruous. It also meant she had money. Megan ran a hand through her hair, and walked confidently towards the woman.

"I'm sorry, I didn't catch your name when we were talking inside."

The woman smiled as she opened the car door.

"My name is Cora. Why don't you hop in on the other side. I'll drive so you don't have to waste your gas."

Megan smiled and closed her eyes as she realized how perceptive and kind this woman was. It was hard for her to drive clients all around the valley when gas prices were so high. Stan Phillips, her broker, had a strict rule. No riding in cars alone with male clients. He hadn't said anything about riding with nice little old ladies. Her gut feeling told her it was okay, so she walked around to the opposite side and climbed in. At five feet seven inches she wasn't short, but she still had to hoist up her skirt, and jump to reach the seat. But as Megan looked around, she knew it was worth it. The thing was a tank. It might look silly in the summer, but this coming winter, Megan knew what she was asking Santa for. No way was this thing getting stuck in snow. The creamy white leather interior didn't hurt either.

"Wow."

Cora laughed heartily as she drove quickly out of the parking lot and headed north.

"It's a gift from my son. My car got stuck last winter. I sat in my car and practically froze to death before a very kind police officer came to my rescue. When my son heard about it, he had a conniption fit. I call it the beast, so I hope everyone's calling me beauty."

Megan chuckled politely and wondered if someday she would have a son as thoughtful as Cora's. How sweet.

"So why don't you tell me a little about your home before we get there? I can start taking down some information now, and save you some time."

Cora glanced at her and grinned.

"Driving isn't work time, Megan. It's fun time."

Cora popped in a CD and began singing along to an opera Megan didn't even recognize. Megan felt the tension ease out of her shoulders and stomach as she was completely charmed by this crazy woman. All she knew about her was that she had a bad habit of staring, she had a great son, and she couldn't sing at all. Megan decided to like her on the spot.

Less than fifteen minutes later, Cora drove up to a small, gray stucco home near the center of Orem and pulled into an even smaller garage. Megan clenched her hands and she closed her eyes, waiting to hear the clash of the car running into the wall. As Cora turned the engine off, Megan blinked in surprise. She hadn't thought it possible.

"Hey, you should see me pack a suitcase," Cora boasted proudly.

Megan eased the door open a couple inches and barely squeezed out. Cora had gotten the monster SUV inside the poor little garage, but there was no room for anything else. Not even a cobweb.

"Come on in, and we'll eat some lunch before I give you the big tour. It's only leftovers, but they're pretty good. I made enchiladas last night, and I made way too many. I don't know why I do, but every time my son comes to town, I tend to go overboard. It's just in my nature."

Megan followed Cora and noted all of the major points of the house. Nice, well-kept yard, beautiful mature maple trees, shrubs and roses. Stucco house, so no upkeep, perfect. Small windows, but plenty of them. Cora opened the front door for

Megan and followed her in, while Megan continued her internal monologue.

Good carpet, must be new, two tone paint, fireplace with marble mantle. Roomy living room, quaint nook. Small kitchen but state-of-the-art appliances. Very sellable.

Someone had obviously done some heavy duty remodeling, and hired an interior decorator, too. This would be an easy commission. Shoot, if she had seen it before her house had caught her eye, she would have gone for this one. It was lovely.

"Why in the world would you sell this house? It's just adorable."

Cora opened the fridge, smiling over her shoulder at Megan.

"I knew I was going to like you. You have good taste. I will miss it. My husband and I bought it right before my son was born. I've lived here a long time. But my son insists that I sell it. The neighborhood has gotten kind of scary lately. You know, the police had a drug bust on the house down the street just last month. Turns out it was a meth lab. Can you believe it? If my son knew that, he would have carted me out years ago. The only reason I'm moving is because of the grandkids. There really isn't a lot of room for running around. And forget about a pool or a swing set. Nope, it's time I move and give this house to someone who will appreciate it as much as I did. Every time I get sad about leaving I just think of all my grandkids swimming in my brand new pool and playing in the sandbox. I can just see them now."

Megan sat down at the small kitchen table and propped her chin in her hands. Watching Cora putter in the kitchen was such a soothing thing. She felt instantly at home for some reason. Or maybe it was just the thought of impending food that made her so happy. She couldn't even remember the last time she'd had enchiladas.

"So how many grandchildren do you have, Cora?"

Cora stuck the food in the microwave and reached for two glasses.

"To be honest. . . zero. But I have a lot of faith in my son. He's going to come through for me. We made a bargain."

Megan laughed. She was going to have to meet this son. He sounded interesting.

"You are going to be one great grandma. I bet your grand-kids are sitting up in heaven right now, just bursting at the seams to get down here. What lucky kids."

Cora placed the glass of lemonade in front of Megan and turned away to catch the tear that slipped down her cheek. She sniffed quietly as she took the plates out of the microwave. She didn't want to impede the arrival of her grandsons and grand-daughters in any way. She would just have to work faster. The poor things were probably getting impatient.

"We can sign the contracts—I mean, contract—right after lunch. Is that all right with you?"

Megan placed her lemonade carefully back on the table and gazed steadily at Cora.

"You're not playing games with me, are you? I mean, you really want me to sell your home for you, just like that? We haven't even discussed it! How did you hear about me? Was it the Cutlers? Or the Brummels? Or is this one of Dylan's little games!"

Cora looked guiltily down at her plate as she realized she had screwed up. She had to play this just right or everything could fall apart.

"I'm sorry if I sound too eager. I've never sold a house before. I guess I just wanted to get it done with as soon as possible so we could get started on my other house."

Megan's frown disappeared quickly as she realized she was being a complete jerk. Why was she being so suspicious?

"Oh just ignore me. It's just that I've never had a client like you before. Usually it's like pulling teeth to get someone to sign a contract. Please forgive me."

Cora's smile lifted her whole face, and she looked almost beautiful. She reached over and grabbed Megan's hand, squeezing it quickly.

"My dear, we're friends now. It's forgotten. Who's Dylan?"

Megan blushed, regretting her outburst even more. She was getting paranoid.

"Just someone who likes to play practical jokes on me every once in a while. He likes to keep me on my toes." And jobless.

Cora nodded her head, satisfied with Megan's answer. "Now, would you like to say the prayer, or would you rather I did?"

Megan didn't know what religion Cora belonged to, so she motioned for her to go ahead.

"Dear Father in Heaven, we thank thee so much for all of the wonderful blessings thou has given me. I thank thee for my health and for my friends. And I thank thee for my dear, dear son. Please bless this food to bring nourishment and strength to us, and at this time, please bless Megan that she will find her way, and that she will find happiness and joy. In the name of Jesus Christ, Amen."

Megan said "amen" softly. "Thank you. Thank you so much."

Cora lifted her fork ready to dig in. "Sweetie, everyone needs all the prayers they can get. Trust me."

Megan devoured her lunch and didn't say no to the second and third helpings. From Cora's beaming face, she knew she had impressed her with her energetic eating style.

Cora just nodded her head and smiled as Megan went over all of the details and the fine print of the contract. Megan knew instinctively that Cora wasn't listening to a thing she was saying. From her dreamy smile, Cora's mind was obviously far away.

"Now, after our appraiser gets back to us with the market

value of your home, we'll get the sign up in your yard. Would you like to set up a time for tomorrow to go look at some lots? Or if you'd like and you have the time, we can fit in a few today. I don't have any other appointments this afternoon." Or all week.

"What? Oh yes! Let's look at some lots."

Megan shuffled the contract and checked all of the signatures. Everything was in order, so she reached for her Multiple Listings book and opened it to the section on land.

"Why don't you tell me a little bit of what you're looking for in a lot? For instance, what area or city are you thinking of? Would you like a small lot or a large lot? Do you want to be out in the country, or near stores?"

Cora's face went blank as she realized she had been so busy daydreaming about grandkids, she hadn't spent one second on thinking where she wanted to be. Megan was going to think she was a real peabrain. She played with her fork as her mind went a thousand miles an hour. What did she want? And then she knew. She had always known. She could see it in her mind.

"Well, for starters, it's at least a third of an acre, you know for the pool and all. And it's up high. I want a view. I want a view of the temple! The new one in American Fork. And I want it to be close to a park. A good one, not one of those run-down pathetic rusty ones. And I want to be close to the mountains. I love the mountains. That's what I want."

Megan wrote this down, unable to hide her grin. She knew the perfect lot. Well, perfect subdivision anyway. The developers had just begun selling the lots last month, and they were going fast. They were in Pleasant Grove, right up on the bench. Megan smiled just thinking of the view Cora would have of the temple. And the park just down the street was world-class. All of the lots were half-acres. The only hitch was restrictions. They were pretty strict on size and exterior.

"Cora, how big of a house were you planning on building?

That can really affect which lot you decide on."

Cora looked surprised at the question.

"My goodness! I need an architect, don't I? I really need to get going on this. Hmm, well, I need my own bedroom, of course, and when my grandkids come to visit me, the boys will need their own room. I'm picturing bunkbeds and blue walls. And the girls, of course, will have pretty little daybeds. Oh, and a room for my son and his wife. So four rooms altogether. And I want a big kitchen, so when I make Thanksgiving dinners I won't be so cramped. I'm sure my daughter-in-law will want to help me cook, so I have to have plenty of room. And I want a pretty little living room, with a piano. I'll learn how to play and then I can give the kids lessons. Hmm. And a big TV room. Have you seen those theater rooms? I want one of those. And a big playroom, that will hold lots of toys."

Cora's eyes were glowing as she talked on and on, not realizing she was describing a palace, not a house.

Megan frowned slightly at the older woman's vast imaginings.

"Cora, let's go at it this way. How much do you want to spend on the house and lot? Have you thought of a price range?"

Cora grimaced, knowing she had to have a serious talk with her son. She was getting into deep water here, and she didn't have all of the information that Megan was expecting. She'd have to stall.

"Oh, money's not really an issue, dear. Why don't we just have fun today? You show me a few lots, just to give me an idea, and then we'll get serious tomorrow. All right?"

Megan closed her briefcase and grabbed her purse. "You're the boss, Cora," she said. "Let's hit the road. I want to show you my favorite lot in the whole world. If I were going to build a house, I'd build it on this lot. You're going to love it, I guarantee it."

Cora followed Megan out of the house, and turned to lock the door. She studied the energetic girl as she strode towards the box that was Cora's excuse for a garage. She liked her. She liked her a lot. She was obviously sweet, although a bit timid or shy, as if she had been hurt before. Her smile was lovely, so unassuming and genuine. She could see why her son liked her. Loved her, she hoped. She was beautiful in a very subtle, classic way that would appeal to her son. But what was it about Megan that was making him act so outrageously? It was a mystery.

Megan directed Cora to drive past three lots in different areas that were nice, but not spectacular. Cora wouldn't even get out of the car to walk around. But as Megan gave her directions to drive to the last subdivision, Cora's face completely changed from politely bored to ecstatic as the elevation became steeper and steeper.

"Oh I can't believe this, Megan! This is wonderful, perfect. I can see the lake and the temple. Oh my heavens, it's gorgeous! I never would have thought it possible. My grandkids are never going to want to go home! They're going to love it here."

Megan felt a burst of pure joy as she watched Cora practically giggling in delight. She may never have a home with a view like this, but helping somebody else attain such beauty was a definite rush. Megan did grow a little concerned, however, when Cora ran up to the "For Sale" sign and started pulling it out of the ground.

"Wait Cora! We haven't bought this lot yet. We have to make an offer and close on it before we can take the sign down. Let's not get ahead of ourselves here. Besides, this is just the first lot we've seen in the subdivision; there are many other lots for sale. Why don't we walk around and pick the very best one?"

Cora scowled at the "For Sale" sign for a minute and then smiled good naturedly.

"I do tend to go overboard on occasion. You'll learn to put up with me, Megan."

Megan took Cora's arm and steered her toward the other lots, noting the pros and cons of each one. But Cora kept looking over her shoulder at the first one she had seen. She had fallen in love, and if anyone else even looked at it, she was going to have a fit. When a car pulled up into the subdivision ten minutes later, Cora sprinted the half a block back, in her high heels, to stand in front of the sign. Megan laughed and gave up.

"Okay, Cora. You win. This is the one and I can't blame you a bit. It is the best. You have to promise to invite me over one night so I can see a sunset from your back porch."

Cora stood in front of the "For Sale" sign while Megan used her cell phone to call the agent listed in the MLS. There had been an offer made on the lot already, but it had fallen through because of financing. Bad luck for them, perfect luck for Cora.

"I set up an appointment for us tomorrow morning at ten to sign an earnest money agreement on this lot. You'll have to put some money down to hold it until we can sell your house. Unless of course you're able to buy it outright?"

Megan glanced back at the Ford Excursion, having no idea what Cora's financial situation was. She could probably buy the property outright.

Cora smiled and relaxed her shoulders. Her lot would be safe. "I'll have to talk to my son tonight, but I'm sure we'll just buy it. I think we'll go ahead and start construction, too. I can't see myself waiting for my house to sell. That would be a waste of time, don't you think?"

Megan smiled, knowing that for most people, waiting was the only way they could do it. The typical person didn't have the money to float the construction of a new home, while making mortgage payments. That took a lot of money. Or faith.

"Let's call it a day then. I know you probably want to get home and call your son."

Cora glanced over at Megan as they drove back down the mountain and smiled. Megan had no idea that she had just helped to pick out the place where she and her future children would be seeing countless sunsets. Hopefully. Now, if only her son could "close the deal."

"Megan, why don't I just drop you off at your house instead of the office, and then I can pick you up for our meeting at ten?"

Megan glanced up from the notes she had been writing down, raising her eyebrows.

"Now, Cora, you are too thoughtful. Clients shouldn't have to drive their real estate agents anywhere. It should be the other way around. I don't want to put you out."

Megan studied Cora for a moment. What a sincerely nice person. This had been her lucky day and she had a lot to be thankful for. Now she wouldn't have to go crawling to her mother for money.

"Cora, if I had one wish, it would be that my kids could have a grandma like you."

Cora's lower lip began to tremble, as Megan went back to her notes. She had no idea where Trevor had found this girl, but if she had anything to do with it, she wasn't letting her get away.

Chapter 6

"Well?"

"Well what?"

"Did you sign the contract?!"

"Of course I did, you ninny. She's exquisite and the perfect mother for my grandchildren. I'm just a little curious about how, where, and when you met her. I wouldn't mind some details you know."

Trevor threw his briefcase onto his mother's bright, floral-print couch and collapsed comfortably on it. His mother had signed. He'd been on pins and needles all day wondering what his mother would make of Megan. Even worse, he had feared that his mother would recognize her from his high school days. He could still remember his mother pointing out Megan at one of the football games and criticizing her hair and makeup. He wouldn't be the one to remind her of that.

"That's for me to know and you to find out."

Cora put the halibut she was marinading back in the fridge and turned to face her son with hands on her hips.

"Excuse me? Instead of slipping in a few little tidbits of how wonderful my son is, I could be telling her about the time you shaved your hair off for Halloween and had to be rushed to the emergency room for a blood transfusion and stitches. Or there was the time you and your friends got caught by the bishop stashing all of the hymn books in the nursery toy closet."

Trevor winced at the memories but couldn't help laughing anyway. "You know, you should have been a gangster or a lawyer, Mom. You have the killer instinct. You just have to go for the throat, don't you?"

Cora wiped her hands on her apron and advanced towards

her son menacingly. "There's something you're not telling me, isn't there, Trev? What's the mystery here?"

"Okay, I'll be honest with you. She doesn't even know me. I saw her for the first time in ten years last week. Satisfied?"

Cora stepped back with a blank look on her face. She must have missed something. "What?"

Trevor closed his eyes and asked himself yet again, what he had been thinking to involve his mother.

"Forget it, Mom. You signed the contract. For better or worse, you're helping me win Megan over. I know this isn't how it normally works, but from the moment I laid eyes on her at the reunion, I knew deep down that she was for me. I don't really want to go into all of the details of why, when, or where though. Let's just deal with the present. Okay?"

Cora sat down next to her son, who was looking at her with wary eyes. "That's fine. I'll leave all of the details alone if that's the way you want it. But you do have to answer one question. It's just yes or no."

Trevor sighed and closed his eyes.

"What do you want to know, Mom?"

"I don't even know if this is possible, given the time restraints, but do you love her?"

Trevor didn't answer right away. He reached for his briefcase and took out a small black velvet jeweler's box. He turned and opened it, showing his mother what lay inside. Resting on the satin lay a one-carat diamond surrounded by emeralds, set in a wide gold band.

"Grandma Riley's ring. I had Blaine get it out of the safe for me today. I still remember when you gave it to me after her funeral. You said, 'If you can put this ring on the finger of a woman half as wonderful as your grandma, then you'll be the happiest man alive.' Mom, Megan is wonderful. But right now, I can't give you a yes or no answer. All I can do is tell you that I very much want to be in love with Megan. I think there's a good chance I could be."

Cora reached out and picked up the ring and stared in surprise.

"Honey, there's being prepared for every possibility and then there's going overboard. Are you sure you aren't jumping the gun here a little? Like you said, you haven't seen her in about a decade. People change. And this is eternity we're talking about. This isn't some business deal. This is life."

Trevor stared at the ring in his mother's hand and knew she was right. Marriage these days wasn't something you gambled on.

"Mom, just hear me out. I know I'm acting crazy here but for the last year or so, I've been fasting and praying that I would be led to the right woman. Someone who will be a good wife and a good mother to my children. I kept getting the answer to go home. Everytime. So here I am. I'm even transferring my offices here. If the Lord is going to answer my prayers, then I have to do my part, right? And then, I get the invitation to my high school reunion and something tells me to go. I've felt the spirit before Mom, I know what it feel likes and I know I was supposed to be there that night. The minute she walked through the doors, I felt . . . I felt amazing. As if a great weight had been lifted off my shoulders. Here's this stunning woman, practically a stranger and yet I just knew that she was the answer to all my prayers. I don't know what the future holds in store for me. But if the spirit is telling me that this is my path, then I'm going to do my part."

Trevor took the ring back from his mother and smiled earnestly into his mother's eyes.

"So from where I'm sitting, being prepared is the only way to be."

Cora leaned over and kissed her son gently on the cheek.

"Well, that answers my question, doesn't it? If you're listening to the spirit, then that's all I need to know."

Trevor gently placed the ring back in the box and put it safely back in his briefcase. His mom was on his side and all it took was telling her the truth. He'd have to remember that.

"Come on Trev, we have just enough time to go look at my lot before I put the fish in the oven. I'll drive."

Trevor grinned as he followed Cora out the front door. Something had definitely put a spring in her step. She was practically skipping.

"This must be some lot."

"It's the Garden of Eden, and my genius of a future-daughter-in-law found it for me. I hope it's not too expensive. You didn't give me a price range or a budget."

Trevor smiled at his mom as he leaned over to kiss her on the cheek. "You don't have a price range. You're getting what you want. It's as simple as that."

Cora patted her son's cheek and reached for her CD collection. Trevor pulled his own CD out of his suit coat pocket, beating his mom to the player.

"La Traviata?" she said hopefully.

"Nope. Variety keeps you young. Let's try a little Billie Holiday, shall we?"

Cora frowned. She loved belting out her opera, but as the bluesy, romantic lyrics flowed over her, she felt something sad and romantic answer back. It almost made her wish for something. A something she couldn't put a name to.

After walking over every square inch of the lot, Trevor agreed, it was going to be very close to heaven. The two stayed up late into the night, talking and making plans for the house. It reminded him of when his mom would stay up late with him on a science project or before finals. It was so nice to be on the giving end. And it was about time for his mom to start receiving.

Chapter 7

Megan was surprised when Cora pulled out a checkbook and wrote out the check for the full amount of the lot. The other realtor looked taken aback as well. As she walked out of the office, the first thing Cora wanted to do was go rip the "For Sale" sign off her lot. Megan laughed at this, wanting to go with her, but she had responsibilities back at the office. She had to take all the phone calls and walk-ins for the next four hours until Dean came in, so Cora reluctantly agreed to take her back to the office.

"I'd like to take you out to dinner to celebrate, Megan. I can never thank you enough for finding me the most beautiful lot in the world. Do you like Italian? What do you think? I'm kind of craving Mexican."

Megan climbed up into the Ford Excursion and couldn't help laughing with happiness. It was amazing sometimes, how Heavenly Father blessed your life through the actions of others. Not only was she making six percent commission off the lot Cora just bought, but she would make a six percent commission off of Cora's house when it sold, and also the future house through the builder. Life was looking up for her.

"Cora, you don't have to take me out to dinner. I'm sure there are tons of other people you'd rather go out and celebrate with."

Cora drove towards Megan's office, not bothering to put in her new CD. It was too new and special, and she wanted it all to herself for a while.

"Not really. My family only invites me over for special occasions and birthdays. And my friends still have all of their families around, so nights are out. It's a good thing I like my own company so much, huh? So what do you say, Chinese?"

Megan smiled gratefully at Cora. "You got yourself a date, Cora, but I insist on treating. What would you say if I took you to The Roof for dinner?"

Cora looked in surprise over at the young woman who was laughing in anticipation. Had she been wrong? Did Megan have money? She hadn't thought so.

"I won a gift certificate last week and I've been scratching my head over who to take. You'll be perfect, and I won't even have to worry about whether or not to kiss you good night. What do you say?"

"I say I'll pick you up at six."

Chapter 8

Megan heard the knock on the door and frowned at the clock. Cora was twenty minutes early. She must really be eager to celebrate. But when Megan opened the door, she was surprised to see Drew Jarvis.

"Brother Jarvis, what a surprise," she said forcing a smile.

The older man smiled apologetically and asked if he could come in for a few minutes. Megan felt a familiar knot of dread start to form in her stomach, but she shut the door and motioned toward a faded Deseret Industries arm chair. If he asked her over for dinner again, she'd just have to tell him that she just wasn't interested. She hated situations like this.

"First off, I'd like to say how sorry I am-"

The sudden ringing of the doorbell interrupted Drew's speech, and Megan leapt up from the couch to get the door. Any interruption right now, would be very welcome.

It was Cora and she looked great. She was wearing a slim black skirt and a short sleeve gray cashmere sweater.

"Oh, you have company. Should I come back in a little while? I am a little early," Cora asked.

Drew looked flustered, but stood up from the chair and walked over to Cora.

"Hello, I'm Drew. Please don't leave on my account. I was just here to ask a favor of Megan."

Megan was a little confused. A favor?

"Of course, you should stay, Cora. Don't be silly. What can I do for you, Brother Jarvis?"

Drew sat back down and cleared his throat a few times.

"Well, I've discussed the situation with my three daughters

at length, and they're convinced you're the only one who will do."

Megan looked down at her toes, worried now about what Drew might say in front of Cora. The only one who would do what? She braved a glance at him and dared to ask, "Do what?"

"Well, the reason we've been inviting you over for dinner so much lately, is because—as you know—my wife died a couple years ago, and since then, the girls have had only me to depend on for advice. Well, since they've become teenagers, it's gotten a trifle more complex. The girls had a meeting and came to me with the idea. We were wondering if we could do a little trade. We invite you to dinner, and you act as a beauty and social consultant for my daughters. They looked over the whole ward and decided that you were the one they wanted. What do you say?"

Megan smiled in acute relief. "Of course I will. Dinners or not, I'd be happy to help. Besides, it sounds like fun."

Drew stood up beaming, acting much more relaxed. He had come through for his girls, and they would be happy to see him tonight. "Wonderful. I'll have the girls call you and set everything up."

Megan showed Drew to the door, and turned in time to catch an odd expression on Cora's face. She looked as if she had been zapped.

"Cora?"

"Who was that man, Megan? He seems familiar to me for some reason, but I can't place him."

Megan picked up her purse and sunglasses and followed Cora out the front door. "Drew Jarvis. He's in my ward. He has five children—three girls, and two little boys. He's a professor at the community college, he's very nice, and—I'm glad to report—wonderfully uninterested in me."

Cora stopped in mid-stride.

"Wonderfully uninterested?' What do you mean, Megan?"

Megan, who was used to the Excursion by now, hopped up easily into the passenger side.

"I mean, I was terrified he was looking at me to fill his wife's shoes. Thank goodness he only needs me on a consultation basis. That's about all I'm cut out for."

Megan smiled as she said it, but knowing it was probably true still put a shadow in her eyes. Cora put one of her favorite CDs in the player and sang her heart out all the way to Salt Lake. Then as they reached the downtown area, Cora switched to light classical. Megan was relieved by the change and hoped her ears would stop ringing before the night was over. She knew what she was buying as soon as she got her commission check. Ear plugs.

It was a quick trip up to the top of the Joseph Smith Memorial Building, and even quicker to find The Roof. It was a Tuesday night, so fortunately it wasn't too crowded. They both loaded up their plates and headed for their secluded seats by the window. The view was spectacular, but Megan had eyes only for the food. She hadn't seen such food in years. Since her wedding breakfast to be exact. Poor Cora, she was going to keep her here all night long if that's what it would take to eat her fill. She was in heaven, and she never wanted to leave.

"So Megan, what do you say to me setting you up on a date? I know the perfect guy. You'll just love him, I know it."

Megan choked on her jumbo shrimp and had to spit it into a napkin before she fully recovered. "Excuse me? What did you say?"

As if unaware of Megan's mishap, Cora took a delicate bite of her calimari before meeting Megan's eyes, which were still watering.

"Well, you're such a wonderful girl, I just thought it might be fun for you to hook up with someone just as great. I can vouch for him. He's perfectly harmless. And good looking. I think he's gorgeous."

Megan took a cautious sip of water to test her throat. It seemed to be working again.

"No."

Cora put her fork down.

"Why?"

"Because."

"Because why?"

Megan laughed and stabbed a forkful of salad.

"You're stubborn, I can tell. But I have to warn you, I'm determined to take a long and refreshing break from dating. I haven't had a date worth dressing up for in at least three years."

Cora frowned, not even hungry anymore. This wasn't turning out the way she had imagined it. How could an attractive, nice young girl not want to date anymore? Did her son know this already? Was that the reason for this peculiar charade?

"Why do you hate men so much, Megan?" Cora asked.

Megan looked aghast, swiveling around to see if anyone had over heard Cora. "Please don't say it like that. I'm not militant or anything, and I don't hate men. I just have bad luck with them. That's all. I've always been a complete failure at relationships. You name it, father, mother, friends, employers, everybody. But especially men. Trust me, you'd lose your appetite if I told you all of my horror stories."

Cora put her elbows on the table and massaged her forehead with her fingertips. She was going to need some aspirin. Maybe if she played the money card, Megan would come running. It couldn't hurt, and she wouldn't even blame Megan. She was so poor, she was bound to jump at it.

"This guy I know is very rich, Megan. Very. You could eat in restaurants like this every night if you wanted to. And if it worked out, and you two got married, then just think of what kind of lifestyle you would have. No more worrying about money. That's worth the gamble, isn't it?"

Megan thought about trying the shrimp again. Maybe Cora would stop talking if she saw that her victim had her mouth full. Nope, no such luck. Cora looked determined, and not in the least put off by Megan's reluctance to bite at the bait she was dangling.

"Even worse, Cora. Money ruins people. Unfortunately, I know first hand. It turns people into slaves. They have to have this, and they have to have that. And if that person has a better this, then you have to run out the next day and get a better one. I lived practically my whole life playing that game. My parents still are, and they're molding my little sister to play right along beside them, just like they did me. I couldn't handle that type of life again, thank you very much. I'll stay poor and grateful for what I have."

Cora grew quiet and thoughtful. Well, she wasn't a gold digger, that was for sure, but there was more here that Megan wasn't telling. Cora was determined to find out. But in the meantime, she had to set Megan up with her son. It was the first step towards her grandchildren getting here, and they had been waiting long enough.

"Yes, men can be obnoxious, tiresome, and exhausting, but what about kissing? When's the last time you had a really good kiss? Hmmm?"

Megan laughed softly and shook her head as she remembered Trevor's kiss from Saturday night. It really hadn't been that bad. She could still see the deep red imprint of her hand on his cheek and hoped it had faded.

"The last man who kissed me was a complete moron. The kiss wasn't half bad, but there's more to life than kissing."

Cora figured she'd just have to pull a play out of her son's book then. Bribery was a very handy tool when it came to maneuvering people.

"I'll make a deal with you. Even though my nephew is a realtor, I'll refer all my friends to you, if you just go out on one date with this young man. What do you say?"

Megan looked at Cora as if she had just turned into a cockroach.

"Uh uh. No way," Megan said confidently. "You're so nice, you'll refer them to me anyway. Gotcha!"

Seeing Cora's expression, she had to laugh. But she had made a rule not to give into emotional manipulation when she moved out of her mom and dad's house, and she wasn't going to start giving into it now. But she did feel a little sorry for Cora. She was so set on matchmaking, that it was ruining their evening. Megan sighed as she realized that she was going to let Cora set her up on a blind date. Ugh!

"All right, Cora. I have a deal for you. It's the only deal you'll get from me, so take it or leave it. I will go out on a date with this fabulous young man of yours, if you agree to do the same. With a man of my choosing. We'll double date. What do you say?"

While she was waiting for Cora to speak, Megan looked down at her plate and realized she had eaten everything in sight. She was ready for seconds. But when Cora said nothing, Megan looked at her curiously.

"Cora?"

The older woman was speechless. She had been beaten at her own game, and she couldn't do a thing about it. Her? Go on a date? The last man she had dated had been her husband, and he had died more than twenty-eight years ago. She had been so busy working and raising her son that she had never had the time or the desire to date. Sure, she could have dated after Trevor had moved out, but by then, who cared? She was forty-seven years old. Who would want to go out with her? Just the thought had her face turning red. She couldn't do that to Jack! Her Jack was probably in heaven right now, looking down at her shaking his head. She was sealed to Jack for eternity. No way could she go out on a date with some stranger. But what would Trevor say if she told him she had failed? Her grand-children! They were waiting for her! What should she do?

Megan tilted her head, waiting for a response from Cora. For such a verbal person, two minutes without saying a word seemed an eternity.

"Cora? Did I say something to offend you? We can drop this dating stuff if you'd like. There are many more interesting things to talk about. Like a zillion."

Cora rubbed her hands over her face and tried to smile up at Megan, who stood up by their table with her plate in her hand.

"Don't worry about me, honey. You just go fill up your plate again. I'm still working on mine."

Megan walked towards the dessert table, wondering what in the world had floored Cora. A little of her own medicine had evidently gone a long way.

Chapter 9

Cora drove up to her house, and by the lights on, knew immediately that Trevor was inside waiting for her. Waiting to hear good news. And all she could do was disappoint him. She sighed as she expertly pulled into her garage and took much longer than needed to find the front door. What could she say? She knew what she wanted to say. She wanted to tell him that everything was set, all he needed to do was show up and the girl of his dreams was his. Or there was the truth. Cora put her hand on the doorknob and took an extra breath of courage. Before she could exhale, Trevor was swinging the door wide open for her.

"Mom! I've been waiting forever. How'd it go?"

Cora closed her eyes, knowing what she was going to say and knowing that he wasn't going to like it. Cora laid her purse and keys down on the hallway table and walked wearily towards her rocking chair.

"I'm sorry, Trevor, but I don't think I can set you up. You're a big boy now, I'm sure if you try really hard you can do this all by yourself. All it takes is a little effort."

Trevor stood over his mom, who was now sitting down. She looked . . . intimidated?

"What happened tonight, Mom? Why the sudden change? You were all gung ho about setting me up this afternoon. Tell me, did Megan do something to upset you?"

Cora looked up at her son and burst into tears. Forget the lot, the house, the grandkids, everything. She just couldn't go on a date. She'd never be able to look at Jack's picture hanging on her bedroom wall again.

"She won't go on a blind date unless I go on a blind date, too. She wants to double date."

Trevor hadn't seen his mother cry since he graduated from college. What was this? Trevor knelt down by his mom's side and put his arm around her. As he patted his mom's knee and told her it was all right, it came to him. His dad. That was what this was all about. Trevor shook his head and frowned. He wasn't sure he wanted his mom to go on a blind date with some strange guy either, but if it meant seeing Megan again. . .

"What about going on a date scares you, Mom? I've been around a lot of men, so I can fill you in. There's no reason to be scared. Occasionally they're smelly, but I know this from personal experience. They usually shower and brush their teeth before picking up dates. Let's see, oh and the conversation thing isn't that scary. It's actually kind of fun. Sometimes it even beats old reruns of Bonanza. Every now and then anyway. And they usually pay for dinner and the movie, or whatever. But, if you're scared of that part, then I'll make sure you have an extra twenty in your purse in case he thinks you're going dutch."

Cora raised her red, bleary eyes up to meet her sons and reached for his hand, not even cracking a smile at his joking.

"What if he tries to kiss me, Trevor? The last man I kissed was your father, and I've always wanted to keep it that way. That's the scary part."

Trevor leaned over and kissed his mom on the forehead, very gently.

"Mom, you don't have to go on a date, ever, if that's the way you want it. I don't want you to be scared or sad. I'll find some other way to work this out. Why don't you go on to bed. You look tired. Do you want me to fix you some hot chocolate?"

Cora shook her head sadly. She wouldn't be dreaming of dark-haired grandchildren that night. The only thing she could think of was how she had failed her son. He had needed her, and she had let him down.

"I really messed things up, didn't I, Trev?"

Trevor reached into his pocket and felt the box holding the diamond engagement ring. He couldn't seem to put it down.

"Mom, just so you know, my last three dates didn't feel the need to kiss me good night. I didn't even get a hand shake from the last two. You know, Megan did say she wanted to double date. You would never even have to be alone with the man. I can be the one who takes you home. But it's up to you. Like I said, I don't want you to be scared about this in any way."

"Poor Megan, the last man who kissed her was a complete moron. What are my chances?"

Cora got up from her rocking chair and walked into the kitchen, thinking about what Trevor had said. It might work if she was with a group of people. She could pretend she wasn't even on a date at all. Maybe.

Trevor watched his mother walk into the kitchen, and felt a slight tremor of foreboding. Megan couldn't have meant him. Surely.

Chapter 10

Megan floated throughout the next day. There was nothing that could get her down. She had a client! A crazy, wonderful client. Her luck was definitely changing. Okay, so the phone hadn't rung once in the past two hours, but she had hope! Her floor time was from one to six and she was ready for anything. Megan was so energized (or was it bored?) that she found an old bottle of windex and went to work on the windows. She was only half-way through when the the phone finally rang. Megan sprinted across the office and picked up the phone on the second ring.

"Western Realty, this is Megan Garrett, can I help you?"

"Megan, this is your mother. Your father is having some people from a magazine over tonight for dinner. We need you to be here. They're doing a story on him for Business World. This is very important to him. We need to show them a united front. Can you be here by five-thirty for pictures? Dinner will be served at six. Oh, and wear something nice. All right, dear?"

Megan glanced at the clock. It was five and her floor time wasn't up till six. She expelled all the air in her lungs, not looking forward to the tug o' war that was about to take place.

"Sorry, Mom, if you had told me even yesterday, I might have been able to swing something, but I can't leave the office till six. I can probably make it for dessert if you'd like."

Trish Garrett didn't like the word "no." She never had.

"That's just not acceptable, dear. After all we've done for you, don't you think you could do this one thing for your father? After the fiasco of your wedding, don't you think you've embarrassed him enough for one lifetime? I really think showing up tonight would be in your best interest. After all, it would be a start in making things up to your father."

Megan opened the top drawer of her desk, and reached to the far back for her bottle of Tylenol. Her mother had a bad habit of causing her pain.

"If it was so important to him that I be there, why am I just now finding out about it?"

Megan tried to keep her tone of voice even and courteous, but she felt a sudden burst of anger at the attempt to humiliate her into submission. She knew anger never helped any situation, so she concentrated on a memory she had of her mom when she was a little girl. She had been lost at the mall, and her mom had found her, crying and upset. And she had made it all better. It was the best memory she had of her mom and it came in handy at times like this.

"Oh, I'm sure I sent you an invitation, Megan. You probably just misplaced it. You can't blame me for your poor organization."

Her mother was lying. She had a really bad habit of doing that.

"Is Linette going to be there?"

There was a pause from her mother. Obviously she had hit the nail on the head.

"As a matter of fact, Linette just informed me that she won't be able to be here till eight."

So that was the real reason behind the sudden invitation. She had to come up with a daughter quick, and she had been desperate.

"Tell the magazine that pictures will be after dinner. Goodbye, Mom."

Megan hung up the phone and wondered why she was going. She wasn't even really a part of the family anymore. But there was always hope, and she couldn't let that die. Not yet, anyway.

Chapter 11

Megan drove up to her family's home in the Riverbottoms and sat in the car as the cramps in her stomach grew worse and worse. This was not going to be fun. It never was. She forced herself to get out of the car, and glanced down at the pantsuit she had been wearing at work all day. Dean had been late, so she hadn't been able to go home and change. It wasn't that bad really, if you didn't mind a mile of wrinkles.

"Megan!"

Megan jumped out of her skin. She turned to see who was calling to her out of the trees, and saw her sister motioning for her. Megan looked up at the house quickly and then ran over to her sister.

"Linette, why aren't you inside? Mom's going to kill you."

Linette was in the shadows, but Megan could still see the pouty expression on her face. Her mom and her little sister could have been twins. They looked the same, and they had very similar personalities, which of course meant they didn't get along at all.

"Meg, I wouldn't go in there if I were you. I'm not. Let's take off! We can go see a movie or something. Or. . . we could go get something to eat."

Megan smiled and put her arm around her sister. After moving out, she hadn't been able to spend as much time with Linette as she would have liked. Mostly because of her parents. To them, Megan was just a reminder to them of how they had failed. But she should have made more of an effort.

"How about I go in, just for pictures, and then I'll sneak out, and we can go rent a video and pig out on popcorn. Oh, but you probably have classes tomorrow. Maybe Friday?"

Linette grabbed onto Megan's arms, with surprising strength, considering how skinny and frail she looked.

"Give me your house key, and I'll just wait for you at your house, okay?"

Megan looked up at the house, knowing what waited inside for her, and shrugged. It might help to have something to look forward to. And it looked like her sister needed someone to talk to.

"Fine. There might be a bag of popcorn in the pantry. You're welcome to anything you find. I'm just sorry there isn't more. I didn't go shopping this week."

Or last week.

Linette grabbed the house key Megan held out to her and ran for her car, a sporty little Mazda. Megan frowned as she looked closely at her sister's departing figure. She wasn't just thin. She was emaciated. Megan watched with worry on her face as Linette drove away. Then she turned and walked quickly towards the door to her parent's home. The sooner she got this over with, the sooner she could get to her sister and ask her why in world she was starving herself.

Her mother was at the door to greet her.

"I knew you would do this. I tell you someone's going to take your picture and you automatically pick the ugliest thing in your closet. You used to have such good taste, Megan, I don't know what has happened to you. Hurry upstairs before anyone sees you, and I'll give you something of mine to wear. I can't believe this."

It was so much easier to have good taste when you had plenty of money to back it up with. Megan followed her mother up the stairs meekly without saying a word. That's the way her mother preferred her targets. Silent.

"Here, try this on. You're taller than me, but thank goodness you didn't get all soft and plump like your Aunt Audrey.

Oh forget it, the color clashes with your eyes. I still don't know where you got those green eyes. I guess it will have to be the silk. Oh well, I haven't worn it in months. It never suited me anyway. Hurry, Megan. We'll be waiting for you on the deck."

Megan watched the door shut firmly on her, leaving her alone in her mother's bedroom. It had been a long time since she had been in this room. Her mom had redecorated since then. It was now an Amazon jungle. Whatever the style was, Trish Garrett was the first one in line. Megan glanced at the outfit her mother had flung at her and fell helplessly in love. Megan had always loved clothes. At one time it had practically been an obsession, fed by the demands of her parents. Now, clothes were just a dream to her, completely out of reach. Except this dream felt amazingly real. It was a pale mossy green silk sheath that matched her eyes. Completely simple and utterly perfect. Megan shed her wrinkled suit and shimmied into the silk with a sigh of delight. Well, at least the dress offered something good about the night.

Megan followed orders and reported to the back deck in less than five minutes. Her father and mother were in a corner discussing the details of the article with someone who was obviously in charge. The photographers were setting up their equipment. If she was lucky, she could be out of here in half an hour.

"Megan, good! Thank goodness you're not as slow as your sister."

Megan felt the critical eye of her mother assess her, and was surprised when her mother smiled.

"Well, I suppose that dress does suit you. Very becoming actually."

The sudden rush of happiness reminded her of when she was a teenager all over again. Her parents had been so stingy with compliments and unfailingly generous with criticism, so whenever Megan received a compliment, she had been in heaven. She could just about count on her fingers how many times that had happened. There was the time she had made the cheerleading squad. The time Dylan had asked her to be his girlfriend. When she had been voted most popular. Oh, and she couldn't forget the time she had been praised for her good sense in getting engaged to Dylan. That had been the last time. She'd have to go home and write this one down in her journal.

"Where do you want me, Mom?"

Trish looked over at the photographer for her cue, and then motioned Megan towards her father. The backdrop of the picture would be the sunset. She couldn't help remembering the promise Cora had made to invite her over to see one of hers. She smiled, thinking of what her parents would make of Cora, then frowned, wondering what Cora would make of them.

"Hi, Dad."

Lane Garrett turned and raised one arched brow at his eldest daughter. The disappointment in his eyes always cut her like a knife whenever she walked into his view. She had once thought that his disappointment would fade eventually. He had made sure that it hadn't.

"I'm surprised you showed up tonight, Megan. This is Alex Wrainright. He'll be taking our picture."

After all of the introductions were made, the group picture was taken which took only ten minutes. Now they were taking single shots of her father. Megan smiled in relief. She loved it when she was wrong. Maybe she should splurge and pick up some ice cream for tonight. Linette looked like she could use it.

"Listen, Mom, I've got to run. I've got company coming over tonight. I'll get the dress back to you when I see you next, okay?"

Trish twitched her nose and shook her head.

"I'll never wear it again. You can keep it or give it to Deseret Industries, I don't care."

Megan watched as her mother hurried over to talk to one of

the caterers who was preparing to leave. No good-bye, no thank you. Nothing.

"If you wouldn't mind staying a few more minutes, I'd like to get a quote from you."

Megan turned to see a man staring at her intently. He must be the writer. Megan pasted on a pleasant smile and tried not to glance at her watch. Linette had never been known for her patience. Megan didn't want her taking off before she had a chance to talk to her.

"No problem."

Megan followed the man into the empty living room and sat down on the opposite couch.

"What do you think of your dad's business?"

Lane Garrett ran a publicity company for actors, public officials, and sports figures. Since Hollywood had discovered Utah, business had been booming.

"I think he's done an amazing job."

Megan had never been included in anything resembling a business conversation with her father, so she really had no clue what his "business" entailed.

"Let me rephrase the question. What do you think of the way your dad runs his business? There have been allegations against your father by other publicity firms that he's just in the business of mudslinging. One company stated that since it was impossible for your father to make his clients look good, his only other option is to make everyone else look bad. What can you say in his defense?"

Megan sat back, and clasped her hands tightly. She was in way over her head here, and she wasn't sure what to do. For all she knew, these allegations were completely true.

"Would you mind telling me which company it was you just quoted?"

The man flipped through his notebook quickly.

"I've got it right here. It was Carlisle and Beckstead, Inc."

Megan felt a rush of cold air pour into her lungs. Dylan had ruined her financially, she couldn't let him ruin her father. He had to be stopped.

"You know, you should really check your sources. For one thing, Carlisle and Beckstead, Inc., is not another publicity firm. They're an advertising agency. And I'd think you'd be interested to know that the reason they're spreading rumors about my father, is because almost eight years ago, the two companies were going to merge. When the deal fell through, there were a lot of hostile feelings on their part. They're just out for revenge, and if you print that garbage about my father, then you'll be doing what you just accused him of."

Megan jumped up from the couch. She had to find her dad and tell him this wasn't a cover story he wanted. This was a hatchet job.

"Hold up, Ms. Garrett. Where are you going? I wasn't finished asking you all of my questions."

Megan turned in the doorway to scowl at the journalist. Now she knew why the world looked down on them so much. They had no regard for anyone.

"What else could you possibly have to ask me?"

"I just wanted to know what you thought of Strike, Inc.'s failed takeover? Can your dad handle another attack like that one, or will he have to give in next time?"

Megan felt her temples begin to throb viciously, as she wondered what in the world she could say to that? Her dad was a stranger to her, and his company was even more so.

"Didn't you know? My dad never gives in. He'd rather die."

Megan turned and walked out of the room quickly. She found her dad chatting with one of the camera crew.

"Dad? Do you have a minute?"

Her father's face changed completely in less than a second, going from carefree and friendly, to cold and austere. Megan was usually scared off by the frost act, but this was too important.

"I thought you had already left. What do you need, Megan?"

The camera man got the hint and found an excuse to leave the room. She was alone with her father for the first time since she told him the wedding was off. From his disappointed expression, it looked as if he was remembering the last time, too.

"This is a hatchet job, Dad. That journalist is going to write horrible things about you in this article. You need to put a stop to it right now."

Lane sneered politely down at his daughter before turning to add more ice to his drink.

"Not that you would know, but the first rule in this business is, 'No publicity is bad publicity.' Besides, why would you care? When have you ever worried about anybody else's feelings?"

Megan's shoulders slumped in defeat, as she turned silently and walked quickly out of the room and out of the house. She had only been trying to help, but her father wanted nothing from her. She hadn't been able to come through for him before, so he had written her off. She meant less than nothing to him now. And the realization felt like it would kill her.

Megan drove home in a trance, completely forgetting about her sister in her misery. But when the front door to her house opened, she nearly jumped out of her skin. There was her sister, standing in the doorway, looking very worried.

"I told you."

"Linette, please tell me that Mom and Dad treat you better than they treat me. Please tell me that you have a wonderful, loving relationship with them."

Linette moved back to let Megan walk past, then rubbed her arms as if she were chilled as she followed Megan into the kitchen.

"Why would you think I would be any different than you? Surprise, surprise, I'm just as unlovable."

Megan felt the tears run down her cheeks as she grabbed

her sister in a hard hug. "I love you, Linette, and you better believe me, because it's the truth"

Linette wiped the tears from her own eyes and handed her sister the popcorn. "Come on. Get out of that dress and relax. The popcorn is stale, but at least it's covered in butter."

Chapter 12

"Why are you starving yourself, Linette?"

The girls were both laying on the floor in front of the TV in their sweats, with their hair up in ponytails, munching away happily. The old packet of microwave popcorn wasn't too bad if you ignored the unnatural after taste. But Megan couldn't wait any longer; she had to know.

Linette instantly sat up to put distance between them acting offended because of the question, but after seeing the sincere concern on her sister's face, she crumbled.

"It's the one thing I can do. I let them down with my grades. I let them down with my looks. I could never be as pretty as you. I let them down constantly. Mom was always telling me I needed to lose weight if I wanted to be pretty, so one day I listened to her. It turns out it's the one thing I can do right. For the first little while, Mom and Dad acted as if they were so proud of me, and it felt really good, you know. But then, they started criticizing the size of my nose. Mom even made an appointment for me with a plastic surgeon. It was then that I realized I'd never be good enough for them. I'd never make Dad proud of me. So I finally quit trying."

Megan rolled over and tugged her emaciated sister over to her side. At twenty-three, she weighed as much as a fourteen-year-old. Megan ignored all of the sharp angles of her sister and cuddled her like she did when they were younger. The two sat on the floor together with their arms around each other for a long time.

"I don't want you going back there. I can't stand the thought of you being anywhere near people who don't see you as the amazing, beautiful, incredible person that you are. It just makes me sick. You know, Linette, you don't have to take it. You can live wherever you want to. What would you think about moving in with me? I've got two extra rooms, and a monster of a dog that doesn't care what color your hair is or what your waist line is. And there's me. And I love you more than anything or anyone. What do you say?"

Linette moved away from her sister and turned to face her. The hope of freedom had her hands shaking as she reached out and grasped Megan's arms.

"Don't say it, if you don't mean it, Meg. Because I don't think I can last much longer. I tried moving out before, but they told me they would cut me off. But if you'll stand by me, I'll do it."

Megan jumped up from the floor and ran to the phone. She quickly dialed her mom's phone number, smiling at her sister bracingly.

"Hello, Mom? . . . Hi, just wanted you to know Linette is here with me, and as a matter of fact, she's moving in with me tonight. I'll be over tomorrow to pick up her things. . . Yes, I can do this. She's not a juvenile, and I will make sure she graduates from college. That's only a month away. . . No, I'm not doing this to hurt you. . . No, you can't press charges against me for kidnapping. Good night, Mother."

Linette got up on her shaky legs and walked haltingly over to her sister and raised her hands to Megan's face.

"You do love me, don't you? I thought you did, but I wasn't sure because Mom and Dad didn't. I didn't know if anyone could. We'll be together, Meg. Just you and me. We'll be happy."

Megan hugged her sister and couldn't help wincing at the bones she could feel through Linette's back. This was her fault, too. If she had been more involved with her sister's welfare, regardless of her parents, she would have made sure things hadn't gotten this far. Now it was up to her to get her sister help.

* * *

After Linette had gone to sleep, Megan snuck out to run to the grocery store. She had to get some decent food in her sister. No way was she feeding Linette a half a bowl of bran flakes, which was practically all she had left in the house to eat. She'd have to use her credit card, but with the commission off of Cora's lot coming in soon, she could handle it. Besides, her sister was worth it.

She loaded her cart full, but gulped when the receipt totaled $98.27. Megan smiled as she put all the groceries away, though. She had so much food, she could probably invite someone over for dinner now. Cora would be nice. Cora would be nice to her sister.

Megan hummed happily as she got ready for bed. She had a busy day tomorrow, but she knew she had the strength to do it. And she was going to do it all with a smile on her face. First off, she was going to get all of her sister's stuff while she was at classes. And then, she was going to confront Dylan. Megan looked in the mirror and reminded herself to smile.

Chapter 13

Getting the clothes had been easy. All of Linette's things were in the driveway in boxes. It took two trips with her car, but she did it. She and Linette were roommates now. The thought had her smiling, and her eyes twinkling. It was just like Cora's prayer. She was finding her way.

Megan looked at the pile of boxes and decided to leave them for Linette. Besides, she had one other appointment today. As she drove towards the offices of Carlisle and Beckstead Inc., and remembered all of the times she had driven there to take Dylan to lunch, or to show him color samples for the reception. She especially remembered the time she had sped across town to show Dylan the brochure on Italy. She had always wanted to go and had thought a honeymoon there would be perfect. Megan blinked as the thought hit her. If she had gone through with the marriage, she would be getting ready to celebrate her eight-year anniversary. Just remembering the way Dylan had looked at her at the reunion had her shivering. She hated to think of what her life would have been like.

Self-righteousness had her walking quickly up to the front desk and asking to see Dylan. How dare he say such horrible things about her father! She was going to make him leave her and her family alone once and for all. She just wasn't sure how.

"Megan, what a surprise."

Megan turned to see Dylan standing in the doorway of his office, wearing an exquisite midnight blue suit that matched his eyes. He was always one to make an impression.

"I need to speak to you, Dylan. I have a few things I want to talk to you about."

Dylan's mouth turned into a hard, thin line, but he motioned her in. It was now or never. Megan entered his office briskly, standing squarely in front of Dylan's ebony desk, too scared to sit down. She waited impatiently as he walked more slowly to his desk and leaned one hip on the edge.

"I was laid off for no reason from Royden and Powell just because your uncle was my boss and I was willing to take that. But I've paid my dues to you, and now you won't leave my father alone. He has never done anything to you. If you don't stop, I'll hire a lawyer and sue you for slander. I swear I will."

Dylan moved quickly away from the desk, turning his back to her and staring out of his office window. His shoulders looked so tense, it made her wince.

"Megan, it's too hard to look at you. I want you to leave."

Megan's nose wrinkled in confusion. What? That was all he had say to her?

"I'm not going anywhere until you promise to stop telling reporters horrible things about my father. I want you to leave me and my family alone. This is over and done with, Dylan. It was over eight years ago. Wouldn't it be a relief to just get rid of all of this garbage and get on with your life?"

Dylan turned around suddenly, causing Megan to step back in fright. She never had known what he was capable of.

"It will never be over until I know why, Megan. It's been eight years and you still haven't had the guts to tell me why you left me at the temple. Can you even imagine what if feels like to be in the temple, waiting for your bride, and then to be told she wasn't coming? I had to go into the sealing room, by myself and tell all of my relatives and friends that there would be no wedding. You killed me and left me for dead that day, and I'm still dead inside. You're the one who has to end it, Megan. All you have to do is tell me why."

Megan shook her head in confusion. It almost sounded as if Dylan was the one who had been wronged. Something was definitely off here. Megan walked over to a chair and sat down before answering.

"What are you talking about, Dylan? I gave Taffie the letter to give to you. It explained everything. After she told me about everything that went on at your bachelor's party, I knew I couldn't go to the temple with someone who would do those kinds of things. If anybody's heart was broken, Dylan, it was mine."

Dylan turned and picked up a paperweight and threw it against the far wall, causing Megan to jump nervously. She was ready to run to the door, but Dylan grabbed her and whipped her around to face him with only inches between them.

"There was no letter and there was no bachelor party. What are you talking about?"

Megan pushed her hands against Dylan's chest, but he refused to release her.

"Taffie told me. Her brother Alan was there. She called me the morning of our wedding, and told me everything. All about the strippers and the alcohol. She told me everything you did. How could you expect me to go to the temple with you the very next day? I told you all of this in the letter. Why didn't you read it?"

Dylan let Megan go suddenly and walked furiously around the room, running his hands through his hair.

"Taffie never gave me any letter, Megan. And there was never any bachelor's party! My two older brothers flew in for the wedding that night and we spent the evening going over their mission pictures. I stayed up until eleven o'clock with my mom and my dad and my two brothers talking about what an amazing thing eternal marriage was. I couldn't stop talking about how lucky I was to have you, Megan. That was my bachelor's party. All you had to do was ask me."

Megan's knees gave out and she slumped to the floor. This couldn't be real. Was it possible she had believed a lie for eight long years? No wonder Dylan was furious at her. He had gone eight years not even knowing why he had been left at the altar. Megan shook her head slowly. This was so wrong. She could have been married for the last eight years. She could have had children. She could have been happy.

Dylan stood back, looking at Megan strangely. He couldn't believe what she was saying. If he did, then that meant his wife was to blame, and that would mean his marriage was a complete sham. Dylan walked behind his desk and sat down calmly. He had to get control of himself.

"All right, Megan. I want you to go over everything that happened. Everything you believe happened. Don't leave out any details."

Megan pulled herself up to stand and walked shakily over to the chair she had discarded. She smoothed the hair away from her face and wiped the tears from under her eyes. Could she dredge up everything again? She took one look at the despair in Dylan's eyes and knew she had to, for his sake. If he was right about what had happened, she had a lot to make up for. She spent the next hour explaining everything. At the end, she felt so drained, she didn't know if she could even stand to leave. She wouldn't be surprised if Dylan called security and had her thrown out.

"She told me you were seeing someone else. She told me you had fallen in love with another man while I was on my mission," Dylan said.

Megan rubbed her hands against her eyes, smearing her makeup, and making her look even more defeated. She held up her ringless left hand and looked Dylan in the eyes.

"There was never anyone else, Dylan. Not then and not since."

Dylan slammed his fists against his desktop and moaned as if he had been stabbed. Megan jerked to her feet, and reached out, but pulled back slowly, as she realized she couldn't comfort him. She had no right to.

"Dylan, I need to go. My sister is moving in with me today, and I need to meet her back at my house. I don't know what to say. I came here wanting an apology from you, and instead I find out that I'm the one who should be begging your forgiveness. I'm so . . . sorry. It's amazing what a few little lies can do to change your life, isn't it?"

Dylan raised his head as she walked towards the door.

"Wait."

Megan turned her head, with her hand on the doorknob. He sounded so sad. She hated to leave him.

"What can I do, Dylan?"

"You can wait while I fix this mess. You can wait for me."

Megan didn't pretend to misunderstand him. She knew exactly what he meant. Dylan was thinking there was still a chance for them. Whatever Taffie had done, she couldn't encourage him to break up his marriage.

"I'm sorry, Dylan."

Megan walked through the door, and was proud of herself when she only glanced back once. He looked grim, but determined. He looked like he was ready for combat. She almost felt sorry for Taffie. But not quite.

Chapter 14

Megan got into her car and drove out of the parking lot. She couldn't seem to concentrate though. Instead of houses and cars she kept seeing Dylan's face. She couldn't believe what she had put him through. No wonder he acted the way he did. He was justified. Poor Dylan. Megan looked around in surprise as she pulled into her driveway twenty minutes later. The strange thing was, she couldn't remember getting there. Megan slowly got out of the car and walked into her house. She and Dylan would have had a house by now. Probably a big showy thing, but still, she would have had a husband to share it with. And children. Megan shook her head and stared into space, thinking about what might have been.

Linette walked out of the kitchen and could tell immediately by the expression on her sister's face that something was troubling her greatly.

"What's wrong? Did Mom and Dad call the cops on you?"

Megan came out of her trance and walked past her sister into the kitchen. She threw her purse on the table and collapsed in a chair. She would have preferred the cops to Dylan's revelation.

"Worse. I went to see Dylan. I found out everything, Linette. Will you grab the yellow pages? Look up Prozac, and see if you can get someone who delivers, please?"

Linette rolled her eyes and sat down next to her sister. She patted her back awkwardly, not sure what to do.

"Trust me, they don't deliver, I've tried. But if you want something to cheer you up, dinner is already made, and I'm not much of a judge, but I think it's going to be pretty good."

Megan looked at her sister suspiciously and sniffed the air. Holy cow. Someone had been cooking. Italian!

"You've got to be kidding me! You got carry-out for me? I knew there was a reason I liked you so much. Let's dig in."

Linette laughed and shrugged her shoulders.

"I didn't have to. Someone named Cora came by with bags of food. I've never seen anything like it. She forgot the Parmesan, so you just missed her, but she said she'll be back in ten minutes. She's amazing, Meg. I really like her. Talking to her is like talking to a real person. And she says she'll hire me to decorate her new house! Can you believe it? I graduate in less than a month, and I already have a client."

Megan and Linette grabbed each other by the arms and jumped up in the air together, laughing and whooping. Megan tilted her head towards heaven and smiled her thanks. Cora was turning out to be one huge blessing.

Cora walked right in, witnessing the sisters very apparent joy without even knowing the reason, she joined in the laughter. She knew it had been a good idea to just invite herself over. And she was never wrong.

"You two girls are a sight. You can't tell me the thought of lasagna has you this excited."

Megan walked over to Cora and hugged her silly, causing the older woman to turn red with embarrassment.

"Cora, you are a darling and just the person I needed to see on a day like today."

Megan leaned in closer, so Linette couldn't hear and added, "Thank you for making my sister so happy. You're an angel."

Cora winked at Megan and walked over to the stove to finish up. "Why don't you girls set the table and I'll get this masterpiece out of the oven."

Megan and Linette exchanged glances of glee and rushed to grab the plates and forks, not even bothering to look for napkins. The smells coming from the oven were too divine.

Cora proceeded to load up everyone's plates as much as she could without having food spill out onto the table. Linette looked a little alarmed by so much food, but Megan knew it was good for her to be in a normal eating situation where people weren't counting all of your calories for you. She needed to realize that eating was good. And when Cora cooked, it was even fun.

"Linette, would you mind saying the prayer?" Megan asked innocently.

When they were younger, Linette had always copied every-thing her older sister had done. She had even decided to take the missionary discussions along with her older sister and get baptized. Megan had a suspicion that's where her sister's religious education had ended.

Linette seemed startled by the request, and looked down nervously. She didn't want Megan to know that since she had moved out, not one prayer had been said at home. Linette was a little rusty when it came to heavenly communication. She stole a glance at Cora and winced, noticing that her eyes were already closed, waiting for the blessing to begin. She cleared her dry throat and closed her eyes.

"Dear Heavenly Father, umm, . . . hallowed be thy name. Umm. We're thankful for this food that Cora so kindly prepared for us. She seems really nice. Umm. I'm thankful for my sister who took me in when she didn't have too. And I'm grateful she loves me. In the name of Jesus Christ, Amen."

Linette opened her eyes quickly, scanning the table for any snickers of amusement. Meg smiled at her sweetly, and Cora was already grabbing the spatula. Well! That hadn't been so bad. Maybe she could handle this religious stuff after all? Now for a little dinner conversation.

"So why'd you go see Dylan? I thought you kicked him out of the picture years ago."

Megan glared at her sister and looked at Cora pointedly. She hadn't wanted to go into it in front of Cora. She liked Cora, and didn't want her eyes opened to the sort of person her real estate agent really was. But Cora was all ears. Megan sighed, and then decided why not. It might not hurt to get the older woman's advice so Megan told them everything.

"And I think he wants me back. He told me to wait for him. I think Taffie's the one getting kicked out of the picture this time."

Cora's mind was in a jumble. Poor Megan! And poor Dylan, whoever he was. And poor Trevor!! If Dylan had his way, Megan would be off the market in the time it took to get a divorce, and Trevor would have to return that beautiful ring to storage. So much for taking things slowly. They were headed for the fast track as of right now. Cora grimaced and knew what she had to do.

"Rule number one, Megan. Stay away from married men. I know there are special circumstances here, but regardless, that's a whole new mess you don't want any part of."

Megan silently agreed, and smiled when her sister nodded her head vehemently.

"I know, Cora, I know. I just feel so guilty, like I should be doing something. Maybe I should wait for him."

Cora took a deep breath and dove in.

"I know what would get your mind off of Dylan's marital troubles. . . . a romantic evening of dinner and opera. What do you say? Can I set you up?"

Megan's mouth quirked up on the side as she shook her fork at Cora.

"The question is, are you up for a romantic evening?"

Linette looked back and forth between the two women who looked like they were up for anything but a romantic night out.

"Hey, I am. Forget about setting Megan up, set me up. I could definitely use a night out on the town."

Cora chuckled and grabbed Linette's hand and squeezed it.

"Tell you what, sweetie, why don't we all go out together?

And I'll find you a handsome young prince, too. It looks like it will be blind dates for all three of us."

Megan grimaced across the table at Cora, who had a similarly pained expression on her face. Linette, on the other hand, was all smiles.

Chapter 15

Cora sighed inwardly as she drove up to her house and saw the lights on. Again. Trevor was beginning to make a habit of waiting up for her. It would have been sweet, except she knew darn well it had everything to do with Megan and absolutely nothing to do with her. But, he was a man with a mission and he was here to get her report. At least she had some good news to go along with the bad this time. Their percentages were getting better.

Trevor didn't even bother for his mother to reach the front door. He must have been looking out the window, because he was jogging out to meet her before she could even get out of the garage.

"How's my beautiful, wonderful, perfect mother doing this evening? I hope you had a good time?" Trevor asked hopefully, praying that his mom had come through for him. After discussing the ins and outs of the dating scene with his mother over lunch, he had been sure that she felt comfortable going on a double date with him. He had flat out promised her there would be no emotional bonding and absolutely no physical contact between her and any date Megan could scratch up.

Cora smiled sympathetically at her son. He looked exactly like he had as a little boy right before he opened his birthday presents. So blissfully expectant. Boy was he in for a surprise.

"Yes, before you pop, you have a date this Saturday."

Trevor laughed out loud with happiness and picked up his petite mother and whirled her around the yard, not caring what the neighbors were making of the spectacle.

"Trevor Riley, you put me down this instant! That's not the

only news I have for you. You can wipe that grin off your face because you have some serious competition to deal with."

Trevor frowned and lowered his mother to the ground, feeling all of his triumph melt away. Competition? He crushed the competition in the business world. But in his personal life, that was another matter all together.

Cora winced at the defeated look on her son's face and took him by the hand as she had when he was a little boy and led him inside the house.

"Honey, you better sit down for this."

Trevor's shoulders slumped even further as he collapsed on his mother's couch. He was ready for the worst.

Cora stood in front of her son, and looked him straight in the eyes.

"Sweetie, Dylan Carlisle is planning on divorcing his wife and picking things up with Megan where they left off eight years ago. But don't feel too bad, you do have a date with her this Saturday."

"Dylan! No, I can't believe this," Trevor shouted.

Cora patted her son on the shoulder before sitting down in her rocking chair. She told him everything Megan had related to her about the situation.

"I can't stand that jerk. If you could have seen the way he treated her when they were together, you would know. And what did Megan say? Did you get the impression she was still in love with him?"

"Honestly? I really don't know. I do know that she feels so guilty about what happened eight years ago, she may be willing to do almost anything to make it up to him. Don't worry, though. She told me she was absolutely going to stay away from him while he's still married to Taffie. She's a good girl. But after the divorce is final, your guess is as good as mine. We've been taking things way too slow here, Trev. You've got to speed this up if you want your girl. If you ask me, you have approximately two months to get that ring on her finger. Dylan has a huge advantage. He has a past with her and he has her guilt. All you have is me."

Trevor groaned before grabbing his cell phone. He pushed the button for Blaine and waited two seconds before the connection was made.

"Blaine. You've got a date Saturday night . . . No this isn't your bonus for the year, but if you impress everyone with how debonair you can be, I promise you that your bonus will be much larger than usual . . . Just meet me at my mom's house and then we'll all drive over together . . . Yeah, she has an Excursion. . . Oh, and see what you can pick up. My mom wants opera, but I'd rather go to a play. Check around."

Trevor hung up the phone and caught his mother's eye.

"If she doesn't fall in love with me Saturday, then it's going to be an uphill battle the whole way."

Cora clicked her tongue and shook her head. Her son was in for an eye opener. Love wasn't a business deal. It was a complete gamble.

"I couldn't stand your father on our first date," she informed him.

Trevor groaned again.

Chapter 16

"Do I look all right, Meg?"

Megan turned around to see her sister standing in her bedroom doorway. Her shoulder-length brown hair was up in a twist, with tendrils of hair framing her thin expressive face. The dress was loose and flowing, hiding the fact that she needed to gain at least fifteen pounds. Her cheekbones stuck out about a mile, but her eyes were sparkling with excitement and anticipation. She looked radiant.

"Linette, you know you're gorgeous. You're not the problem here, I am. I seem to have forgotten how to apply eyeliner."

Linette rolled her perfectly made-up eyes and walked over to join her sister in front of the mirror. She wiped the smudged eyeliner off expertly and grabbed the tube of liquid eyeliner instead. She applied it as if Megan were a canvas.

"There. Now you look better than me and my date will probably be staring at you all night."

Megan tried not to blink as she let the liner dry, but couldn't help sticking her tongue out.

"If anyone is caught staring at me, it's usually because I have something in my teeth."

"What a joke. Here I am, Art Deco standing next to the Mona Lisa. What are you complaining about? You're beautiful; you always have been and you always will be."

Megan frowned critically at her reflection in the mirror, not believing it for a second.

"Whatever. I'm the one Mom had to get the contacts for, bleach and perm my hair, and take to the tanning salon twice a week. Mom never tried to turn you into a barbie doll. You already were one."

The two sisters laughed at their reflections as Megan reached for a tube of cranberry lipstick. Linette's mouth began to droop as her old and relentless insecurities reared up again in the form of memories.

"Mom just knew I was hopeless. Besides, I knew in my heart I would never have big hair like yours. There was no reason to try. You better hurry, though. Cora will be here with our dates in about fifteen minutes. I'll bet you a million dollars she's right on time."

Megan smacked her lips and shook her head, making her hair fall more naturally. She would just have to do. She tilted her head to the side and really looked at herself. Was Linette right? Did she really look okay? She had gone from caring too much about her looks, to not caring enough probably. It was only Linette's artistic touch that had her looking so well. The results weren't half bad if she did say so herself. And the green silk dress didn't hurt either. Thank you, Mom. Maybe you gave me two things; my life and this dress. Wait—three things. You gave me a great sister.

"All right, I'm ready. And as long as we're betting, I'll bet you she's at least five minutes early."

The two girls looked over at the clock and laughed as they heard the doorbell ring. Megan felt a little zing of adrenaline shoot through her system as she walked calmly towards her front door. It had been a long time since she had been nervous about a date. She just hoped Cora wasn't going to be too disappointed when things didn't work out. They never did.

Megan ushered Cora in and a young man she didn't know. She secretly hoped he was her date. He looked like a Greek sculpture she had seen once in a museum. His face had definitely been sculpted by a master. She caught herself staring so hard at the young man, she almost forgot about the other mystery man. As he stepped through the door, she felt her stomach drop to the floor.

"Trevor?"

Trevor smiled optimistically and held out his hand to shake hers. When she didn't offer her own, he patted her left shoulder awkwardly instead.

"What are you doing here?" Megan demanded softly.

Trevor cleared his throat, looking towards Cora, as if she could help him.

"I'm Cora's son, Megan. I'm your date for the night."

Megan turned to have his statement verified by Cora. This was too much of a coincidence. This was too much, period.

"Is this your way of getting your five thousand dollar dance? You didn't have to go through the charade of having your mother put her house up for sale. I can't believe you did this. Don't you have better things to do?"

Megan said the words to Trevor, but she was looking at Cora the whole time. She felt completely betrayed. She had believed Cora was her friend. Cora was nothing but a front for her son. How completely manipulative. How sick!

Cora walked uncertainly over to Megan's side and laid a hand on her shoulder. "Megan, sweetie, don't take it like this. We didn't mean to hurt you. I just wanted to get to know you better. Everything is real. You are my realtor. My house is for sale and I am your friend. Trevor does happen to be my son, and yes, he does happen to be interested in you. Is that so wrong?"

Megan glanced at Linette for support, but wasn't surprised to find her sister and her gorgeous date in a corner, talking quietly. If only she could switch dates.

"Fine, let's go," Megan mumbled in exasperation.

She grabbed her purse and walked out the front door, leaving everyone else to follow. She was so furious, she could spit. Right at Trevor. The nerve of him. If he had liked her so much, then he should have asked her out in high-school, for heaven's sake. Even though she had been dating Dylan, he at least could have tried. Well, he had missed his chance. And to think of all the manipulating he had done to get here. It reminded her of her parents. Sick. Sick. Sick.

"Megan, maybe we should talk before we all go out?"

Megan turned to see Trevor standing a few feet away from her, looking slightly ill. The last time she had seen him had been in a darkened ballroom. Outside in the light of day, he was even more handsome.

"Sorry, no time. We have to go pick up Drew, your mother's date. He's expecting us right about now, as a matter of fact."

She didn't add, but couldn't help thinking, the sooner they left, the sooner she could get home. Trevor looked as if he could read her mind and turned a little green even.

The ride to Drew's house was deathly quiet. Linette and her date, Blaine, had apparently caught on that something was very wrong, and were silent. Drew was standing on the street curb with several red roses in his hand, and all five of his kids peeking out the front window of his white colonial style house, grinning and waving. Megan's face cracked into a smile, as she saw that he'd had his hair cut and his suit looked as if it was freshly dry cleaned. Drew obviously looked forward to tonight. Megan wished she were.

Drew climbed into the front seat next to Cora and smiled at everyone as introductions were made. Megan wished she and the other young people would disappear and leave Cora and Drew alone together. Drew deserved a wonderful night out, although she wasn't sure he deserved Cora.

"These are for you, Cora. The first time I saw you, I knew red was your color."

Cora turned an attractive shade of pink and reached over to take the roses. She looked them over carefully, smiling as she smelled them.

"You're right. Thank you so much. I can't remember the last time someone gave me roses."

Everyone turned to stare at Trevor as his voice seemed to

boom out from nowhere. "Sure you do, Mom. Wasn't it when Dad found out you were pregnant with me?"

Megan gave Trevor a look that would have made most men wither. Trevor only looked slightly aggravated.

Drew's smile lost some of its brightness as he turned to face Trevor.

"Your dad was a lucky man."

Trevor grumbled something unintelligible and didn't say another word as Cora drove to the restaurant she and Trevor had picked out for the evening. They had chosen La Caille, a French restaurant that was very exclusive and very expensive. Megan remembered having her wedding breakfast there. She and Linette exchanged queasy looks before following their dates inside. Eating here was going to bring back a lot of memories. She still remembered Dylan standing up and making a toast to her, while she had been composing her farewell letter to him in her mind.

The hostess showed them to their seats quickly, handing them each a menu. Megan made up her mind then and there, she was ordering anything and everything she wanted. She was going home with as many doggie bags as she could get out of him. Besides, he was a millionaire. He could handle it. Megan smiled savagely at the menu, planning what she would be eating for the next week. She and Linette would be eating in style tomorrow. And the next day. And the next.

Trevor felt his stomach flip-flop nervously and wondered if he was going to make it through dinner, let alone the play Blaine had picked out. He glanced at Megan to see if she still looked as coldly furious as she had ever since setting eyes on him. To his surprise, she looked like she was having fun. Maybe she had had a chance to think things through. Maybe she was even starting to see tonight as the romantic night he had planned it to be? Megan's eyes passed over him for only a second, but the temperature change was immediate. She might be having fun thinking of dinner, but the only fun thing she wanted to do with him would probably include instruments of torture and death. Yikes.

"So, Blaine, what do you do for a living?"

Blaine looked away from Linette to focus on Megan's question. He smiled charmingly at her and winked at Trevor.

"I guess you could say I'm Trevor's slave. I'm at his beck and call night and day. Ain't that right, boss?"

Trevor didn't even have to look at Megan to gauge her reaction to Blaine's teasing. He could already tell she believed Blaine's outrageous statement. His mother was looking at Megan, however, and her expression looked hopelessly distraught.

"Remember that bonus we were talking about, Blaine? Why don't you tell everyone here that you're just kidding? We wouldn't want anyone to take you seriously, would we?"

Blaine looked confused. "I wasn't exactly kidding."

Trevor stared furiously at Blaine, planning all the many ways he was going to make him suffer. After everything he had done for the ingrate!

"All right, slave, who sent you to Majorca last month, just because he felt like it?"

Blaine's charming smile was swiftly back in place. "Did I say I minded being your slave?"

Linette and Drew laughed politely but still looked askance at him. This was a nightmare.

Megan chose Cora next. "So tell me, Cora, do you always orchestrate elaborate ways to get your son dates?"

Cora's face turned white and she took a sip of water before looking at everyone at the table. Linette, Blaine, and Drew were looking at her expectantly, sensing the tension at the table. Megan's tone had been pleasant, but her eyes looked as if she wanted to cry.

"No, as a matter of fact, this would have to be the first time.

Maybe if I had had more practice at matchmaking, you would be having a better time tonight."

Drew looked from Megan to Cora to Trevor in confusion. He felt a little uneasy as if he were an actor in a play, but no one had bothered to give him a script.

"There are no complaints here. As a matter of fact, I'd have to say I'm the luckiest man in the whole restaurant."

Cora's thoughts were dragged away from Trevor's dilemma to the very charming and handsome man sitting right next to her. Cora smiled back at Drew and realized that tonight didn't have to be a complete disaster. She had a very charming and kind dinner companion, and since there was nothing she could do to save her son's evening, she might as well enjoy herself as best she could. And to Drew's complete delight, she focused completely on him.

Blaine and Linette had the same idea, and spaced out everyone but themselves after ordering from the waiter. No one even blinked an eye when Megan ordered four entrees. Megan and Trevor looked at each other cautiously knowing they were stuck.

"I'm feeling a little like a fifth wheel here. What about you?" Trevor whispered in Megan's ear.

Megan sighed loudly and threw down her napkin before rising from the table. She could do something about it. There were two other couples here who were more than willing to have a great time. She didn't have the right to put a damper on their evening, just because she had the bad luck to be stuck with a creep. She found the hostess and asked if they could have a different table. Within seconds, they were escorted to an intimate alcove away from everyone and everything. Just the two of them. Alone. Perfect, she thought wryly.

"I hope your sister appreciates your sacrifice."

Megan almost smiled. "She would do the same for me, I'm sure. Just out of curiosity, why did you do all this? You could never bring yourself to ask me out in high school, so why the sudden interest?" Megan asked.

Trevor closed his eyes and wondered what to say to her. The truth? It couldn't hurt him at this point. He was out of the game anyway. He'd just make Blaine return the ring for him. The little slave.

"Because I wanted to in high school, but I was too gutless to do anything about it. I promised myself if I ever had the chance again, I wouldn't waste any time. And when I saw you at the reunion, it just seemed perfect. You're single, I'm single. Why not?"

Megan's mouth hardened into a straight, thin line.

"You don't even know me. This is crazy."

"Sure I know you. Well, a little bit. Okay, I just have a few memories, but why shouldn't that be a good reason to want to go out with you? We were in the same biology class in the ninth grade. We had two classes together our junior year, and our senior year we had government and seminary together. I watched you every day. I saw things most people didn't. You always acted so haughty and snooty around your little clique and they ate it up. They couldn't get enough. You were the quintessential cheerleader. But it was just an act. I saw the time when no one was looking and you went up to Robby Seaver, that boy who had downs syndrome and you told him what a cool guy you thought he was, and how proud you were of him for getting that medal in the special Olympics. You made sure none of your friends saw you, but you did it. But my favorite is the time you stood up to your boyfriend in front of everyone. And boy, did you pay for it. Justin Webster, the one kid everyone picked on, accidentally knocked Dylan's lunch out of his hands, and Dylan of course started to beat the snot out of him. You put yourself right in between them so Justin wouldn't get hurt. You're the one who ended up with the black eye that day."

Megan closed her eyes as the memory of that day came back to her.

"That was an accident," Megan whispered fiercely.

Trevor said nothing as he looked at her with his dark serious eyes. The waiter brought their food at that moment, and asked politely if she would like the chef to keep the rest of her entrees warm in the kitchen. Megan had the grace to blush, but nodded her head regally. Her first pick was lobster. Trevor had ordered steak of all things. Why go to a French restaurant and order steak? It was just as she suspected, the man was insane.

"For a while I couldn't believe it myself. Megan Garrett, the head cheerleader, a nice person?"

Megan cracked the lobster angrily as what he said started to sink in.

"So why didn't you ask me out? I don't believe you were gutless for a second. Not Trevor Riley, seminary president and defender of all goodness and light." Megan looked him square in the face and saw him flinch. She knew exactly why.

"I didn't fit in with your image, did I, Trevor? I bleached my hair and had the best perm this side of Salt Lake. My finger nails were so long and red, you would have rather died then introduce me to your mom. I'm right, aren't I? You were so good at seeing the inside, but you still couldn't get past the outside. You were too good for me, weren't you?"

Trevor sighed and wondered if the evening could get any worse. He had planned to have a wonderful evening. He had hoped to bypass all of the high school baggage and move on to the future. This was not turning out at all the way he had expected it to. There went all of his mom's grandbabies.

"I had a little problem with pride when I was in high school. I admit it. A big problem actually. I thought I had an image to uphold as seminary president. I was on my mission and asking myself why I still couldn't stop thinking about you when I realized what an idiot I had been. Do you remember getting a letter from an Elder Riley in Guatemala?"

Megan had her mouth full at the moment, but nodded her head. She did remember. She just hadn't put Elder Riley together with Trevor the seminary president.

"I thought if maybe we could start writing each other while I was on my mission, then we could get together when I got home. The one time you wrote me back, all I got was one sentence. Don't get worms."

Megan covered her mouth with her napkin, giggling over the memory. If she had only known, she would probably have written a different letter.

"Oops."

Trevor smiled back at the woman still giggling at him. She was stunning when she smiled. Actually she was stunning even when she was looking like she wanted to kill you.

"So did you?"

"Did I what?"

"Get worms."

It was Trevor's turn to laugh.

"Yes, I did and I always blamed that letter for it. The very next day I found out I had parasites in my stomach. I won't bore you with the details, but they almost had to send me home. It was horrible. I still can't eat chicken feet soup without gagging."

Megan was sure he was telling the truth, but couldn't help giggling.

"All right, so maybe you're not the biggest jerk in the world. I can understand wanting to go out with someone you secretly liked in high school, but what I don't get is this huge production. You had your mother set us up on a date! All you had to do was call me on the phone. I'm listed and I did owe you a dance. I would have said yes. Just to warn you though, I'm not sure I'm a good bet right now."

Trevor noticed the shadows appear in her eyes and knew he would do anything to make them disappear.

"Don't sell yourself short. According to my sources, you're quite the prize. Not only are you the best realtor in the world, I believe my mom said you had E.S.P., and you have a gorgeous dog, a nice home and a pretty little sister. There aren't that many women out there who can offer anything close to that."

Megan snorted at the mention of her dog. Maybe Trevor was in the market for one?

"You're forgetting one teensy weensy detail. I'm cursed. If I were you, I'd run for it. Me and relationships don't mix. I'm a disaster just waiting to happen."

Trevor knew Megan was thinking of Dylan. It was as if there was a third person at their table. A very unwelcome third person.

"Did you love him very much?"

Megan's head snapped up as she looked at Trevor in surprise.

"Oh, I almost forgot you had a spy. I should have realized your mom would tell you everything."

Trevor grimaced, knowing he should have done things differently where his mom was concerned. He had thought he was being so clever and inventive.

"Did you?"

Megan tilted her head up in irritation and stared at the lights hanging from the ceiling. Well, it was a night for truth it would seem. She'd never see Trevor again after tonight anyway, so what would it matter?

"Yes, I did. I loved him. I don't know that I was in love with him, but if you grew up the way I did, where there wasn't a lot of affection or even acceptance, having a relationship where someone actually cared about you and looked out for you was amazing. A little overbearing at times, but still comforting. Because of him, I took the discussions and joined the church my junior year in high school. His family really took me in. Wow, was that an eye opener. Family Home Evenings, daily prayer, and scripture study. A family that really loved each other. I have to be honest. I don't know if it was Dylan or his family I wanted more. At the time, my parents thought it was great. Now, I realize that was my dad just making a business deal sweeter. My dad and his dad were going to merge their two companies. Things fell through, though. Oh well, I've always wondered if someone else had asked me out, what I would have done. I guess we'll never know."

Trevor had trouble meeting her gaze. Their lives might have been very different if he had been a little more humble.

"Oh, admit it. If I had asked you out, not only would Dylan have beaten me up, you would have laughed your head off. The head cheerleader and the seminary president. You wouldn't have been able to hold your head up in the cafeteria. Admit it."

Megan pursed her lips, ready to defend herself, and then wondered what her parents would have done if she had come home one day and told them she no longer wanted to date Dylan, the son of one of her father's closest business acquaintances, but that she would now be dating the poor, seminary president. Her mom and dad would have nipped that in the bud as fast as you could say, "no money for clothes."

"I really can't say. I'd like to say that I would have. And besides, Dylan wouldn't have beat you up. Weren't you some karate champion or something?"

"They call it a black belt," Trevor said with a laugh. He reached his hand across the table.

"Let's call it a truce then, shall we? I'll admit that I was a spineless jerk, and that I shouldn't have set this date up the way I did, if you'll admit that yes, I am one of the best looking guys you've ever been out with, and that no, you won't change your phone number tomorrow morning."

Megan laughed and reached out to shake his hand.

"You got it. I won't change my phone number, and yes, you just might be the best looking man I've ever gone out with. But don't let it go to your head."

Trevor's grin was so wide, Megan could tell he would need a clamp to stop smiling.

"And by the way, I'm sorry about that kiss last Saturday. I was just upset that Dylan was trying to humiliate you. It was my dumb way of sticking up for you."

Megan took a sip of water and patted her mouth with her napkin before answering. Holding grudges wasn't one of her favorite things to do. Maybe she should give him a break.

"Okay, Trevor. All is forgiven. But I'm warning you, next time you want a little kiss, ask."

Trevor wanted to jump up in the air and shout, *Hallelujah, she said NEXT TIME!* But he settled for telling the waiter to put all of Megan's untasted entrees into the best-looking doggie bags they could find. He even went so far as to order desserts to go along with all of her meals.

Megan felt slightly mean about all of the food she had ordered, but knew it wouldn't go to waste. It might even tempt her sister to gain a few pounds.

The three couples met outside and waited for the valet to bring Cora's car. Cora and Linette both attempted to catch Megan's eye, wondering where they should go from here. Cora gave up and tapped Megan on the shoulder anxiously, not knowing what her reaction would be.

"Megan, do you still feel up to a play, or would you like us to take you home? Blaine and Linette say they don't care what they do, and Drew and I can take a play in some other time. What do you feel like doing?"

Megan looked around the group for their reactions. It looked as if Blaine and Linette would be happy any place they could talk, and Drew was beaming down at Cora, and would clearly be happy as long as he was with her. Trevor was looking at the ground, but his hands were clenched at his sides. She wasn't sure what to make of that. What did she want to do? She really didn't want to go to a play. Her mind was in such a jumble she knew she wouldn't be able to concentrate. She had started to enjoy Trevor's company. It would be nice to just go for a walk with him. Everybody would think she was an idiot if she suggested that, though.

"Don't worry about hurting my feelings Megan. If you'd rather just go on home, then that's what we'll do. I promise I won't start crying."

Megan's mouth twitched at the thought of Trevor boo-hooing over her. As if. "Well, to be honest, I would rather just go home. I don't feel like a play tonight. Maybe we could pick up a video on the way home and some ice cream, and we could make some shakes or something. And I really need to take my dog on a walk. Would you mind?"

Trevor's face had closed up as she voiced her wish to go home, but at the mention of a video and a walk, his grin was back bigger than ever.

Everyone in the group laughed in relief that the evening wasn't going to end.

Blaine put his arm around Linette's shoulders as he insisted on being the one to pick the movie. Linette's eyes were sparkling and she looked very different from the sad, hopeless girl she had been just a few days earlier. It was amazing what a little bit of love and good food could do for a person. Not to mention a little romance. And she did have Cora and Trevor to thank for that. She turned and smiled at Cora, who walked over to her quickly, pulling her in for a quick hug.

"I'm sorry, Megan. I would never have hurt you for the world. Do you forgive me?"

Megan hugged her back, kissing her on the cheek.

"Of course I do. I was just caught off guard. I didn't know what to think. We're still friends."

Trevor watched his mom and Megan hug and laugh together and wondered if there was still hope for him. Maybe he would keep the diamond ring around for a little while longer yet. He patted the pocket where he kept it and smiled. He could wait another week.

Chapter 17

"I can't believe you named this dog Marjorie. She's more like a Katie or Bridget. Where'd you come up with it?"

Megan tried wrapping the leash around her waist, and then her arm to keep control of Marjorie, but her border collie was impossible. Her walks with Marjorie were always like this. Megan was pulled from one end of her subdivision and back again. Her arms and back always ached the next day.

"I read the book, *Glimpses Into the Life and Heart of Marjorie Hinckley,* and thought it was utterly unfair that I didn't know anyone like her. And if you haven't noticed, I don't exactly have a house full of kids to keep me busy, so I went down to the Humane Society and picked out Marjorie. I knew she would be the perfect companion. I pictured myself going on peaceful walks with her, having her lay at my feet in front of the fireplace while I read a book. You know, all that neat dog stuff. I then woke up to reality. She outright refused to be house trained, so she has to be outside; I have her to thank for the polka dot pattern on my grass. And she was personally offended by all of the flowers and trees I had planted back there, so she took it upon herself to rip them all out. She's quite the companion."

Trevor winced as Marjorie pulled so hard on the leash that it almost took a few of Megan's fingers along with her.

"Give me that before you hurt yourself."

Megan gratefully handed over the leash, and was amazed when a curt "heel" had Marjorie slowing down and keeping pace. Every time Marjorie jumped ahead, Trevor pulled her back consistently and patiently. A half a block later, Megan was actually enjoying her walk. It was a new experience.

"Well, you seem to know all about me, why don't you tell me more about yourself. What have you been up to these past ten years besides getting worms in Guatemala and becoming a millionaire?"

Trevor bent to pick up a broken piece of glass lying in the middle of the sidewalk and stuck it in his pocket. He sighed before answering.

"There's not much to tell really. I came back from my mission and started a computer repair business. I had always loved working with computers and just felt that was where I wanted to be. But in my spare time I developed a computer program that I ended up selling for quite a bit of money. Then it dawned on me. Why don't I forget the repair business and focus on the development of new software programs? After a few years things really started to take off. I've branched out, picked up a few more companies along the way. Sometimes I miss the repair business though, believe it or not. Life was a lot more simple back then."

Megan smiled and shoved her hands into her jeans pockets. It felt good talking to someone. She usually didn't mind being by herself all of the time, but lately she had been feeling sort of lonely. Like she was missing out on something important. Or someone important.

"What about personally? Why didn't you ever get married?"

Trevor paused by a tree to let Marjorie do her business, and scuffed the toe of his shoe across the concrete, as if he were a little kid. He looked very uncomfortable by the question, but Megan didn't feel too guilty. It was her turn, after all.

"There was someone. I was twenty-five, and I had just made my first million. I was feeling on top of the world and I figured it was about time I settled down and started my family. So I went to my singles ward that very next Sunday and began trying to pick out my bride to be. When I did, she looked a lot like you, believe it or not. Well, like you used to anyway. I knew I had made a huge mistake where you were concerned, so I was determined not to be sidetracked by outer appearances. Her name was Bethany. It wasn't hard to get a date with her. She had heard about my company and knew I wouldn't be taking her to McDonald's for dinner. We dated for a few months and then I popped the question. She said yes, and then of course we went and picked out rings. I started to wonder when she picked out the biggest ring available. But what the heck, I could afford it. She eventually dumped me and immediately pawned her ring to start up her own business. She's a successful caterer now and very happy, I hear."

Megan laughed softly, not wanting to believe there was someone as unlucky as she was.

"If I were you, I'd start handing out cubic zirconium rings. You'd save a lot of money that way."

Trevor scowled at her, hoping she was joking.

She wasn't.

"As long as we're talking about our personal lives, do you mind me asking what happened to make you change so much? I honestly didn't even recognize you at the reunion. I couldn't believe my ears when Dylan called you Megan. I had been staring at you from the moment you entered the room. I was racking my brain trying to figure out who in the world this incredibly beautiful woman was."

Megan looked at Trevor quickly, wondering if he was giving her a line or telling the truth.

"What seems sudden to you was gradual for me really. I moved out of the house to go to school, and my roommate, who was there on an academic scholarship at BYU, really opened my eyes. Jeanette was kind. She was genuine and not fake at all. At first I kind of sneered behind her back at her. At the time, I just didn't get it. But she taught me a lot about myself. She taught me that I could be liked for myself, and that I had the right to expect other people to like me for myself, too. She also encouraged me to go to church regularly. I have to admit I didn't go to church as much as I should have after Dylan went on his mission. It was hard for me to go with roommates who had been members all of their lives. I felt like such an idiot as far as the gospel went. They would talk about ideas and concepts that I just wasn't ready for. So Jeanette would bribe me with her homemade brownies to get me to go to the devotionals and firesides with her. When I joined the church, I had a testimony that it was true, but there was just so much I didn't understand. And she helped me with that. I can't believe how much I still miss her. She met and fell in love with an Australian, and that's where they live now. She still sends me Christmas cards every year."

Megan glanced over at Trevor, to see if she was boring him to death, but he just smiled encouragingly at her. Megan smiled shyly back, embarrassed to be revealing something so personal. But it was actually kind of nice to talk about it. She'd never really formed how she felt into words before.

"So eventually I started to find myself layer by layer under all of the junk I had covered myself up with. The real me, the daughter of God, me. I'm not saying people who highlight their hair or wear red lipstick need psychoanalysis or anything. But for me, all of those extras added up to one big shield against the world. Megan grinned suddenly, as she remembered. "You should have seen Dylan's face when he stepped off the airplane after serving two years in Alaska. It was as if the light had gone out of his eyes. For the next three months, he tried to convince me to go back to the way I used to be, but I just couldn't. It took a long time, but this is me. Take it or leave it."

"I'll take you."

Megan was alarmed at his reply. She hoped he was kidding, because she wasn't ready to be taken by anybody—gorgeous, kooky millionaire or not.

"Don't say that."

"If it's the truth, why shouldn't I? Why does it make you so uncomfortable to know that someone wants to be with you? I'll be honest. I think you're beautiful. And I think you're still that kind wonderful person I saw peeks of in high school. I want you to give me a chance."

Megan stopped and stared open-mouthed at Trevor. She was floored, and there he was standing there smiling at her, with her dog at his feet waiting patiently. This couldn't be happening to her.

"You're going way too fast for me, Trevor. Whatever happened to dating a person and seeing if you're compatible with them? Whatever happened to courtship? You sound like you want to go pick out rings tomorrow or something. I just don't work that way."

Trevor thought of his grandmother's wedding ring, and wondered if Megan's green eyes would match the emeralds.

"Don't even worry about the ring, Megan. All I want from you right now is your word that you'll give me a chance. How about this—why don't we go out together for the next month and then at the end of the month, if you want me to hit the road, then I'm out of here. I won't bother you again. A restraining order won't be necessary, I promise."

Megan giggled and began walking again, as she thought about it.

"Will I have to introduce you to people as my boyfriend?"

Trevor smiled reassuringly.

"Absolutely."

Megan laughed, but then realized Trevor was being serious. This guy was a nut, but he was starting to grow on her. And it was just for one month.

Megan looked up and realized they had made a full circle and were now standing in front of her house again. Through the open window she could smell the popcorn that Linette was making for everyone. She still couldn't believe tonight hadn't turned into a complete nightmare. What was wrong with her luck? Was it possible for luck to change? She waited while Trevor put Marjorie in the backyard, leaning up against her railing and staring up at the setting sun. It really was a perfect night. Something that was totally abnormal for a date in her life.

Trevor walked around the corner, and seeing Megan leaning up against the railing, decided patience was a completely boring virtue.

"Hey remember at dinner, when you said all I had to do was ask the next time I wanted to kiss you?" Trevor said as he walked slowly up the stairs towards Megan.

She narrowed her eyes and held her hands out defensively towards him.

"Trevor, you have got to be kidding me. This isn't even the end of our first date, and you already want a kiss? Isn't this a little premature?"

Trevor moved in closer, smiling confidently down into her still narrowed eyes. "You might as well get it over with. This way, you don't have to kiss me later in front of everyone."

Megan's hands dropped momentarily as she tried to figure a way out of the kiss. "Who says I have to kiss you at all? And besides, I really don't think we should rush—" That was as far as Megan got before Trevor bent down and kissed her soundly on the lips. He pulled back briefly, but then came back for another one, when she didn't push him immediately away. He even ventured to put his arms around her waist. When a few minutes later, she did break the kiss, her cheeks were as red as apples. She was blushing!

"Come on, sweetheart. Let's go get some of that popcorn, before Blaine eats it all." Trevor grabbed her hand and pulled her inside, very grateful that this kiss had ended much less painfully than the last one.

* * *

"He kissed you. He kissed you," Linette said in a singsong voice as she picked up the empty popcorn bowl.

Megan knew she was blushing again and glared at her sister's back as they walked into the kitchen.

"How do you know? Were you all peeking out the window?" Megan asked, horrified at the very thought.

Linette laughed as she reached for a glass from the cupboard. "Don't be paranoid. I just happen to be very good at reading people. What would you think happened if someone walked into a room looking like they had been hit by lightening, followed by a man who couldn't stop grinning for an hour and a half?"

Megan giggled, knowing it was true. "Okay, you win. Yes, he did kiss me."

Linette sipped her water and stared at her sister expectantly. Megan rolled her eyes and sighed theatrically. "What!?"

"Tell me. What was it like? Was it like a nerdy kiss or a Brad Pitt kiss?"

Megan smiled and leaned against the counter, remembering every second. "Hmm. Well, it's hard to describe, but if I had to put it into words, and I guess I do, I'd have to say it was a mix of Brad Pitt, Mel Gibson, and a little Russell Crowe thrown in."

Linette laughed and put her glass in the sink. "You're impossible, Meg. Just tell me if it knocked your socks off."

Megan grinned, knowing her socks were definitely still on, which was just as it should be. But there was potential.

"Linette, you said yourself I looked like I had been hit by lightening. What do you think?"

Linette followed her sister out of the kitchen, frowning. "I think Blaine better kiss me on our next date or I'm going to start feeling very jealous."

Chapter 18

Megan watched Brenna wipe ketchup off her little toddler's mouth and then lean down and kiss her, before sending her back to the McDonald's playland. She looked very happy and very content with her life. She looked like everything Megan wanted to be. A mother and a wife.

"Brenna, you are the luckiest woman alive, you do know that, don't you?"

"You don't know very many people, do you?"

Brenna grinned at Megan before eating the rest of her kid's forgotten fries.

"So lay it on the line, Megan. I want all the dirt, I want all the smut, every bit of scandal you can come up with. I want everything a combo meal will get me."

Megan looked down at her double quarter pounder and wondered if it was worth it. She took one more bite, and then nodded. Yeah, it was.

"How much time do you have?"

Brenna glanced at her watch and frowned.

"Thirty minutes before I have to pick up Mitchell from school so give me the short version, but you have to give me half of your fries back."

Megan raised her eyebrows questioningly. Was she serious? She was. Megan pushed half of her fries over to Brenna's side of the table but kept her ketchup. Brenna deserved naked fries.

"Okay, the short version. Well, the morning of my wedding arrives, and Taffie calls me forty-five minutes before I'm supposed to leave for the wedding breakfast. She tells me all about how Dylan went to a wild bachelor's party the night before and had gotten down and dirty with one of the waitresses. She wasn't sure if he had actually gotten drunk, but according to her brother, he'd had at least three beers."

Brenna's mouth fell open in disbelief.

"That doesn't sound like Dylan at all! Sure he could get wild and crazy sometimes, and yes he was pretty much a jerk, but he was always a straight arrow when it came to stuff like that."

Megan looked down at her half-eaten hamburger and stared blankly. She had believed Dylan capable of everything Taffie had accused him of doing. She hadn't had any faith or trust in him at all. That was why she wasn't celebrating eight years of marriage. It was because of her, not Taffie. And here was Brenna, who wasn't even close to Dylan, and she assumed right off the bat he hadn't done anything wrong.

"Well, anyway, instead of believing in him and trusting him, I left him. After the wedding breakfast, everyone was supposed to meet at the temple for the ceremony. And everyone did, except me. I wrote a letter to Dylan explaining how I felt and why I couldn't go through with it, and I gave it to Taffie to give to him. Well, she apparently 'misplaced' the letter. As a matter of fact, I found out just last week, what you already know. Dylan never did do those things. Taffie made it all up."

Brenna shook her head in disgust.

"Does Dylan know?"

"He does now."

"Megan, this is so sad! It's like Romeo and Juliet, except Dylan's still married to the wicked witch of the west."

Megan choked on her root beer, and Brenna looked at her in concern.

"What?" Megan sputtered.

"Sorry, I shouldn't mix up my storylines. Seriously though, what happens now?"

Megan shook her head as she finished chewing her last bite of hamburger.

"Nope, don't go there. Dylan is married to Taffie for better or for worse. His marriage has its problems, granted, but they can work them out if they both try. It's not like I've been sitting at home every Saturday night pining for him. Well, okay, I have sat home most Saturday nights, but that's because I'm a misfit, according to my parents anyway."

Brenna chewed on some of the ice out of her cup as she contemplated her friend's completely messed up life.

"You're right, Megan. And don't get me wrong. I in no way want to encourage you in that direction. I was going more for the revenge against Taffie angle. You know, like painting raspberry jam smiley faces on her car, or blasting her house with primary songs at three in the morning. Fun stuff like that."

Megan laughed and tried to grab one of her fries back from Brenna. Brenna was too fast.

"Remind me never to make you mad," Megan teased.

Brenna stood up and signaled her kids to come down from the slides.

"Well, that was depressing, Megan. Now hurry and tell me something positive so I can leave with a smile on my face."

Megan wrinkled her nose, and then smiled from ear to ear as she stood to join Brenna.

"Trevor Riley kissed me last night and he says he wants to be my boyfriend."

Brenna almost dropped her child as they walked out of the door. "You are lying Megan Garret! There is no way. No way."

While Megan helped Brenna get all three of her young children into their carseats, Brenna stared at her in disbelief. As she slid into the driver's seat, she grabbed Megan's hand.

"All right, I'm starting to believe you. But you have to promise me one thing. Don't let Taffie be your maid of honor this time."

Megan shut the door on her friend, and walked backwards,

smiling as she shook her head. Brenna rolled the window down before yelling, "Come over to my house next week for dinner! I'm not through with you."

Megan laughed and yelled back over her shoulder, "I will if you promise not to steal any more of my food. I'm starving!"

Brenna gave her a thumbs-up and a smile as she drove out of the parking lot.

Megan felt one more empty spot in her heart close up as she realized she could count on Brenna to be a real friend to her. Facing life without friends and family to support you was hard. But facing life with good friends, one great sister, and one exciting male possibility was something to actually look forward to.

Chapter 19

"What is this?" Megan asked Blaine as they stood in her kitchen.

"What does it look like?" he asked. "This is your new cell phone, in case Trevor needs to talk to you. We know you already have one, but this is a Trevor-only phone. He wants to be able to talk to you anytime, anywhere. He's an instant gratification kind of guy. And this is your very own credit card. See, it has your name right here in pretty gold letters. You can use it for anything you want. Need a new dress for tonight's date? No problem. Need to get that cavity fixed? Call the dentist. Whatever you want. Any questions?"

Megan stared at Blaine, who was smiling at her as if this was normal. She glanced once more at the snazzy little cell phone and credit card just within reach.

"I can't accept this. It's too much."

Blaine smiled at her as if she were a child.

"Listen, if you have any questions later, just call me," he said ignoring her modest response. "I've written down my number for you, right there. I've got to run. I'm taking Linette out to lunch. I'd ask you along too, but I find it's so hard to kiss someone when their older sister is watching."

Megan grabbed the back of Blaine's shirt before he could make it out the door. "Just a couple things before you take off, Don Juan. Number one. I see your number written down here, but I don't see Trevor's. Why is that?"

Blaine looked around the kitchen, not meeting her eyes.

"Oh, well . . . that would be, um, probably because Trevor never gives that number out. Of course, he never did tell me expressly not to give you that information. So I guess I could. Do you really want it?"

"Yes."

Blaine winced and then grudgingly wrote the number down next to his on the paper.

"And one more thing. If you're playing with my sister just because you're bored while you're here in town, I'll kill you. You don't know her. She's a little fragile right now and she can't handle someone breaking her heart."

Blaine straightened from the table slowly, looking Megan in the eyes. He wasn't smiling anymore.

"Don't judge me, Megan. And don't automatically assume that I will hurt your sister. I know about the anorexia. She's told me everything. Do you know where she is right now? She's meeting with a counselor to help her deal with why she started starving herself in the first place. And that's not being put on any of Trevor's credit cards either. I'm picking that one up. I like Linette. I care about her. I can't say that I know exactly where this relationship is going, but I'm not going in with breaking her heart on my list of things to do. And it offends me that you think I am."

Megan watched Blaine stalk out of her house without looking back. She had really ticked him off. Megan grinned slowly. Blaine just might do. She walked back towards the table and slowly picked up the credit card. Megan Garrett. Right there in gold letters. Did Trevor do this for all of his girlfriends? There was no way was she putting one cent on this card. If she did that, she would feel obligated to him, and that was no way to start a relationship. She'd just have to pay for his mom's advertising with the commissions she had just received from the purchase of her lot. Poor Trevor. He wouldn't be able to buy her, either.

Chapter 20

Trevor glanced over at Megan as he drove his brand new, sleek silver Lexus onto the freeway and headed towards Salt Lake. She was wearing a conservative formal dress that was probably more than ten years old. It was black and the style was simple, but Trevor knew automatically she hadn't bought it that afternoon. For one thing, he had checked her account, and she hadn't bought anything. Yet.

"So where are we going?" Megan asked.

"Just a simple business dinner. I can't get out of it, so we're stuck. But this will be a good opportunity for you to get acquainted with this part of my life. Don't worry, though. It's just a lot of talking and eating."

Megan felt her stomach cramp up. He was going to introduce her to his business acquaintances! She was going to be on display, just like she had been for her father's business dinners. Megan glanced in the mirror on her visor and wished she had worn a little more eyeshadow, and a darker shade of lipstick. She felt like she was on a roller coaster, and she was just getting ready to go over the edge. It wasn't a pleasant feeling.

"Oh Trevor, I don't know about this. I really don't think I'm ready to meet all of these people. I thought we were just going out for a nice dinner. I don't know anything about you—who your favorite football team is, or what your hobbies are. What if they ask me questions about your business? I'll sound like a complete idiot. All I know is that you like to work with computers."

Trevor frowned in concentration as he listened to Megan vent. Maybe he was throwing her into the deep end a little fast, but that's how he did everything. Fast.

"My favorite football team is the Steelers, I still love karate, and I'm currently in the process of moving my base of operations from Washington to Utah. And if you get really stumped just look confused and say, 'Je ne parle pas anglais.'"

Megan laughed and shook her head in disbelief. He wanted her to pretend she was French. Where did this guy come from?

"I took Spanish in high school. That might work better for me."

Trevor maneuvered the car in and out of traffic quickly and efficiently. Megan sighed as she realized that's pretty much how he did everything. Unlike her. "It's funny. Here I have a degree in business from BYU and I'm nervous about simple dinner conversation."

Trevor glanced at her curiously. "Your degree is in business? What are you doing selling real estate?"

Megan frowned as she searched for an answer. "It's kind of a long story, but basically, I majored in business because Dylan thought it would be good for situations just like this. He pictured us as being this amazingly glamorous couple. He was going to be extremely successful working with his dad, and although I would be a stay-at-home mom, I would stun everyone with my insightful comments at all of the dinner parties we would throw. I still can't believe I did it. I bored myself to tears for four long years, just so Dylan would be proud of me. I guess that was my problem; I was always so busy trying to make everyone proud of me."

It was Trevor's turn to frown. Maybe tonight had been a big mistake. He didn't want Megan to feel like she was just for show.

"So, when things fell apart with Dylan and my family, I was left all alone. No one to make anymore decisions for me. And that's when I chose to go into real estate." Megan smiled for the first time since hearing where they were going. "I love houses.

Big ones, small ones, old ones new ones. I don't know why, I just do. I have to admit that I'm not exactly good at selling them, but I want to be. It excites me, helping families find their dream home."

Trevor glanced over at Megan and studied her profile. This beautiful, educated woman loved selling houses for a living. Maybe it was just her way of getting as close as she could to what she had always wanted herself. A happy home. Or was it a happy family?

Trevor pulled into the parking lot of the Marriott Hotel and handed his keys to the valet before walking around to her side of the car to open the door for her. He noticed she still looked stressed and put his arm around her for a quick hug, and then decided to leave it there for good measure.

"Don't worry, Megan. I'm not going to leave you to the sharks. I'll be with you the whole time. This might even be fun."

Megan felt the solid weight of Trevor's arm encircle her waist and felt some of the tension ease from her shoulders. Fun? She'd be happy if she just survived. As they entered the ballroom of the hotel, Megan couldn't help shuddering as she remembered the last ballroom she had been in. She was amazed to see hundreds of people. This wasn't just a dinner party, this was a "Who's Who" of Utah's business leaders. Megan gasped as she bumped into the governor and almost keeled over when she saw two General Authorities.

'Trevor, you'd better find a corner fast, and stick me in it. I don't think my Spanish is up for this."

Trevor grinned down at Megan and headed over to a group of people who were waving him over. "Just think of all the contacts you'll be making tonight. Think of yourself, not as Trevor's incredibly beautiful date, but as Megan, the best darn realtor in Utah County. Every single one of these people you see here tonight is a potential client. Think about it."

Megan looked thoughtful. Trevor was right, this could be a

good opportunity for her. If she wanted to be a million dollar producer, then this was a good place to start.

Trevor noticed the confidence slowly find its way into the countenance of the woman standing beside him and beamed. She would make anyone a perfect wife. Too bad for everyone else, she was his. He started shaking the hands of the smiling men and women in the group.

"Megan, I'd like to introduce you to some of the most amazing and talented minds of the century. This is Brian Seward, Deirdra Jacobs, Claire Whitby, Nat Barrett and Adam Prescott. Everyone, this is Megan Garrett, my girlfriend."

Megan was halfway through shaking everyone's hands when her smile suddenly faded. Did he have to do that? Megan turned and glared at Trevor, who was looking over his shoulder at the buffet.

"Hey guys, Megan and I are starving—we haven't eaten yet. We'll catch up to you later."

Megan smiled apologetically as Trevor practically pulled her to the other side of the room.

"Did you have to say that? Can't you just say, 'This is Megan.' Did you have to add the girlfriend part?"

Trevor handed Megan a plate and leaned down to kiss her on the cheek sweetly.

"Yes I did. You are my girlfriend and I can't help it if I want everyone in the world to know that I'm the luckiest man in the world. Remember, you gave me a month to make you fall in love with me. Just enjoy yourself."

Megan glowered at Trevor as he piled her plate full of everything he could get his hands on.

"Either you're really hungry, or you're afraid that the chefs are going to cry if you don't eat everything in sight. And I didn't give you a month to make me fall in love with you. I think we need to clarify this situation. I gave you a month to see if we like each other. There's a big difference."

Trevor looked down at his plate critically.

"I'm hungry. And yes, I do get to try and make you fall in love with me. What would be the fun in trying to make you fall in like with me?"

Megan broke down and laughed as she followed Trevor to an empty table set back from everything and everyone and sat down. Trevor was crazy, but at least he could make her laugh. Megan made up her mind to enjoy the night and forget her worries. She was surprised by how relieved she felt.

"Um, Megan? I believe someone you know is making her way over to our table."

Megan put her fork down and turned her head. Who would she know here? Oh no, Taffie Carlisle! Megan groaned. She was doomed to perpetual public humiliation. Poor Trevor. Well, at least he was finding out now how cursed she was. Better now than after the cubic zirconium.

Taffie walked right up to Megan, picked up a glass of water from the table and dumped it unceremoniously on Megan's head. Megan gasped as Trevor stood up in outrage. He wasn't exactly sure what to do since Taffie was a woman, so he sat down again.

"If you come near my husband again, Megan, I'll sue you. Just stay away from us! What did you think was going to happen? So what if Dylan knows the truth now. He's in love with me, not you. You couldn't handle him then—what makes you think you could now? He's mine, got it?!"

Megan looked cautiously around the room. Their table was back away from most everyone, but they still had quite an audience. What must Trevor be thinking?

"Taffie, I know you're upset, but this isn't the place. Why don't we take a walk to the ladies room where we can discuss this in private?"

Taffie laughed in an ugly harsh way and then whistled as loud as she could, drawing the whole ballroom's attention.

"Oh, am I embarrassing you, sweet little innocent Megan? Well good. Your whole family is going to be embarrassed when everyone learns the truth about your daddy. And I can't wait. The mighty Garretts are finally going to be humbled. Your daddy's taken so much from the Carlisles he deserves everything he gets."

Megan stood to face Taffie; it was too much of a strain on her neck to be looking up at the tall, furious woman.

"Look, leave my family out of this. If you have a problem with me, that's fine, I'll deal with that. But my dad has nothing to do with this. He hasn't done anything to the Carlisles."

Taffie rolled her eyes sarcastically, sneering down her nose at Megan. Megan could tell Taffie was horribly upset because there were tears in her eyes. It's hard to sneer successfully when your nose is running. Megan's soft heart kicked in, and she reached out to Taffie.

"Listen, Taffie, I have no designs on Dylan. It's the truth. He's your husband; he was never mine. I know you guys have some things to work out, but that's between you two. Obviously you must have loved him very much to do what you did, and I know Dylan must have loved you if he asked you to marry him. Trust me, I would never try to hurt you in that way. I would never try to break up your marriage. I promise."

Taffie looked at Megan suspiciously and then her face crumpled, letting the tears roll down her cheeks and onto her bright red kimono-style dress. Megan put her arms around the girl who used to be her best friend and hugged her until Taffie's sobs subsided.

"You promise?" Taffie sniffed doubtfully.

Megan grabbed a napkin off the table and handed it to Taffie. "Have I ever lied to you?"

Taffie smiled weakly then shook her head. She believed her.

"Taffie! What are you doing here!?"

The two women turned around at the near shout, cringing

in unison at hearing Dylan's voice. Taffie's husband was furious, and bearing down on them quickly. Megan squeezed Taffie's hand one last time for assurance and then moved to stand behind Trevor's chair. Dylan always had a way of scaring her. She was never sure what he would do, especially when he was mad and he looked ready to explode.

"Go home now. I told you not to show up tonight. What were you thinking? I told you as plainly as I could to stay away from Megan. If I find out that you've gone against my wishes again, you're going to be very sorry. Now leave."

Megan watched sadly as Taffie bent her head submissively and walked quickly from the room, not caring who saw the tears run down her cheeks now. She was obviously devastated. Dylan didn't bother watching her go, his eyes were on Megan.

"I apologize for Taffie. She's been very emotional lately. I hope she didn't upset you too much."

Dylan couldn't help but notice Megan's wet hair and smeared makeup and knew automatically what his wife had done. His eyes turned to slits and his nostrils flared as he fought the temptation to run after Taffie and confront her again.

Trevor cleared his throat, deciding now was a good time to make his presence known. "No apology necessary, Dylan. We'll let you get back to your dinner now. We wouldn't want it to get cold."

Dylan finally noticed who Megan was hiding behind and blinked his eyes in confusion.

"Megan, what are you doing here with him? You can't be here on a date. We decided that you were going to wait for me."

Megan started to walk around Trevor's chair to talk to Dylan, but was stopped by Trevor's hand closing tightly around her wrist. She stayed right where she was.

"Yes, Megan is here on a date with me. As a matter of fact, she's my girlfriend now. So to answer your question, no, she's not waiting for you, and yes, you should go after your wife, because yes, she is your wife and Megan definitely isn't, nor will she ever be."

Megan closed her eyes in horror at Trevor's audacious words. At the moment she'd rather be at her high school reunion all over again. Anything was better than seeing the hurt in Dylan's eyes that Trevor's words had caused. Megan pulled her arm free and walked quickly over to Dylan before he turned away.

"Dylan, I'm so sorry. But what he said is true. I am here on a date with him. Please go after Taffie though. She loves him very much and she's very broken up about this whole mess. I know you two can have a wonderful marriage if you just keep trying."

Dylan looked at her with haunted eyes which made her wonder if she had made the right decision. Should she be waiting for Dylan? No! She couldn't think that way. It was bad enough that he was.

"We need to talk, Megan. Away from everyone else. Just you and me. Will you have lunch with me tomorrow at Caesar's? Meet me there at one o'clock and we'll work this out. Please?"

Megan glanced back at Trevor and wished she hadn't. His face looked like it did the night of the reunion. Hard and cold. He looked furious.

"I'll meet you for lunch if you'll go after Taffie right now and talk to her. Will you do that?"

Dylan grabbed for Megan's hand and held it in both of his before letting go slowly.

"I'll do anything you want me to, Megan."

Megan didn't sit down again until Dylan had left the room. She felt completely drained and slumped down in her chair.

"You know, we should stick to ordering in pizza. What do you think?" Megan said with a tentative smile.

Trevor didn't even smile as he stared at her.

"What did Taffie mean when she said to stay away from Dylan? And please explain what Dylan could have possibly meant by that statement, 'you agreed to wait for me?' I'm a little confused right now."

Megan's hand clenched on the stem of her glass as she stared back at the man whom she had thought was so funny just a half an hour ago. Was this jealousy? Whatever it was, she didn't like it. It was almost as if he didn't trust her. Megan licked her dry lips as she realized she was getting mad at Trevor for one of her own failings. She really shouldn't get upset at seeing the mote in Trevor's eye while there was a beam in her own. She took a quick breath and told herself to be patient with him.

"I went to go see Dylan last week at his office. I thought your mom already told you all of this? I told him to leave my dad alone. I found out last week that he was telling reporters terrible things about my dad's business practices. I just wanted him to stop, that's all. That's why I went to see him. It wasn't to ask him for a date, or to entice him into adultery, if that's what you're thinking. I'm not like that, Trevor. I actually feel pretty bad for him. He just found out that his wife is a world-class manipulator. And yes, he did mention wanting me to wait for him, but I most definitely did not agree to do that. Give me some credit here."

Trevor threw his napkin down on his plate and sighed.

"I'm sorry. I'm just not used to tall good-looking, married men asking my girlfriend for a date right in front of me. I don't know—something about this whole situation just bothers me."

Megan took a napkin and tried to clean up her face. What a disaster of an evening.

"It's not a date, Trevor. Look, why don't I just slip out the back and call a cab? You can stay and mingle with all of your business buddies and I can go home and get cleaned up. What do you say? We can get together and have lunch sometime when there aren't hundreds of people for me to embarrass you in front of."

Trevor shrugged, not caring whether they had made a scene or not. He had gotten past the stage in life where he cared what people thought of him.

"No, thanks, you already have lunch plans tomorrow."

Megan grimaced at the sarcasm and ran her fingers through her wet hair. Maybe the slick look would work for her?

"I'm sorry if the thought of me talking to Dylan upsets you, but we do need to settle this. Besides, I need to ask him a couple questions about my father."

Trevor leaned back in his chair and shook his head in surrender. She was really going to see that jerk for lunch. Of course it wasn't a date, but it was killing him just the same. He didn't want her in the same state with that guy.

"Can I come as a chaperone?"

Megan laughed and picked up her fork. She didn't care if her shrimp was soggy, she was still hungry.

"No, you can't. But I promise to fill you in on everything when you come over tomorrow night. My favorite mini-series is coming on A&E. Jane Austen's *Pride and Prejudice*. Any boyfriend of mine has to prove he can sit through an English romance with his eyes wide open and a smile on his face."

Trevor sat up, grinning back at Megan's flirtatious smile. Little did she know, he had sat wide awake through many board meetings, and had come away very refreshed. Sleeping with his eyes open was one of his specialties. He was the perfect boyfriend for her.

Chapter 21

Megan watched her sister skip around the kitchen smiling at nothing in particular.

"What are you doing, Linette?"

Linette grabbed a cereal bowl from the cupboard and glided over to join her sister at the table.

"What does it look like, silly? It's called breakfast. I have to hurry though; I've got a class at ten and Blaine is meeting me at the gym for a quick workout. He thinks pumping iron will give me more energy."

Megan hid her smile in her bagel. Blaine was true to his word. He was being good for her sister. She was definitely putting him on her Christmas card list.

"You've been seeing a lot of him lately. Don't you think you should be seeing other people too. I mean he's great and all. Very good-looking. But what do you really know about him? What's his family like? Is he LDS? It just seems like you guys are going kind of fast."

Linette shook her head smiling and finished her bite of cereal.

"I'm seeing a lot of him because I like being with him. If I liked being with other guys, I would be. I'm not sixteen, Meg. I'm practically an old maid like you. Oops!"

Linette blushed and looked at her sister from underneath her eyelashes. Megan grinned and shrugged. If she was in New York or California she wouldn't be considered anywhere near an old maid. Utah County was a different story.

"Just for that, you have to do the dishes tonight."

Linette scowled at her sister and stuck out her tongue as if she were sixteen.

"But seriously, don't you think Blaine is just the most amazing man in the world? You know, there's more to him than you think. He lived in foster homes most of his life. He learned about the church when his last foster family took him in. After going to church for a year, he asked to be baptized. His foster family adopted him and had him sealed to them in the temple. Isn't that beautiful? And he went on a mission to Honduras."

Megan choked on her bagel. Blaine? He looked so cultured, so refined! No one would ever guess he hadn't had the best of schools and all the advantages of a wealthy upbringing. He really was an amazing man.

"The thing I can't understand, is what he's doing wasting his time with me. He could have anybody. He's smart, gorgeous, and rich. And the best kisser in the world. Talk about being struck by lightning. But here he is taking little ol' me out and about. I just don't get it. How could I go from being the second unluckiest person, you being the first of course, to being so lucky I go around pinching myself all day. I can't get over it."

Megan frowned at her sister, wanting to shake her.

"You're right, Blaine is amazing, but you're just as amazing, if not more so! You're beautiful, Linette! Get it through your head—you're beautiful. And you're talented. You're graduating with honors, and you've already got jobs lined up. You're smart, you're kind, and you're the best sister in the whole world. Who wouldn't want to go out with you?"

Linette raised her eyebrows, looking doubtful.

"I believe you happen to be one very partial sister, but I appreciate the sentiment."

Megan picked at her bagel, not wanting to make her sister uncomfortable with her next question. She didn't even really have to know. She was just plain curious.

"Um, how's it going with that counselor you've been seeing? Do you like him?"

Linette ate the last bite of cereal before putting down her

spoon and pushing the bowl away. She ran her fingers through her shoulder length brown hair and sighed. She didn't especially like talking about her anorexia. Even to her own sister.

"It's going good. He's really nice. He's the same counselor who helped Blaine through some of his problems when he was a teenager. He makes me feel normal, you know? Like I'm somebody."

Megan smiled across the table at her sister.

"You are somebody, Linette. I'm just glad you're realizing that too."

Linette left ten minutes later, leaving Megan alone with her house, her dog and her thoughts. She really had nothing to do until lunchtime, when she was supposed to meet Dylan. She didn't have any floor time at the office until the next day, and she didn't have any clients to call and check up on. Cora seemed to be happy right now just looking through books of house plans. They hadn't even decided on a builder yet. As far as selling her house, the appraisal had come back, and they were expecting the signs to go up in the next couple days. She had already scheduled the man from the magazine to take the picture of Cora's house to put into the next issue, so she was set. All caught up, and nothing to do but . . . look at her brand new credit card just lying on the counter, practically calling her name.

Megan shook her head and walked into her bedroom, to look through her closet. She had to pick the perfect outfit for her lunch with Dylan. She couldn't help smiling though, as she thought about how happy her sister was. Blaine was turning out to be a really neat guy. Best kisser though? She sincerely doubted it. She already knew who held that title.

Chapter 22

Megan looked down at the clothes she had chosen for her lunch appointment. Faded, junky jeans and her oldest and dearest BYU sweatshirt. She checked out her reflection in the window of the restaurant and smiled. Ugh! She wasn't even wearing foundation and her hair was pulled back in a tight pony tail. She looked like she was getting ready to clean house. Perfect. Dylan would take one look at her and run screaming back to his wife. Megan walked confidently through the doors and didn't even care as the hostess sneered at her while escorting her to the table where Dylan was already seated.

"Hi, Dylan. Hope you haven't been waiting long."

Dylan did a double take of Megan and then smiled slowly.

"You're worth the wait, Megan. I keep telling you that."

Megan frowned as she sat down opposite Dylan. This wasn't exactly the reaction she had been hoping for. She picked up the menu uncertainly and looked at Dylan over the top. He was still staring at her with that dopey smile on his face. Megan put the menu down, folding her hands on top of the table. Enough was enough.

"Dylan, I will never marry you."

Dylan's smile slipped a fraction.

"Don't say that, Megan. If you want, we can discuss marriage after the divorce is final, if you're uncomfortable doing it now. There's no reason to make up your mind this minute. Don't think of yourself as starting a relationship with a married man. Think of it as starting over again with the only man you were meant to be with. Me."

Megan closed her eyes wondering how she could convince

him that this just wasn't going to happen. Ever.

"I'm planning on marrying someone else, Dylan," she said surprised by her own statement. "I don't know what else to say to convince you. I really think you need to focus on keeping your marriage to Taffie together. A temple covenant isn't something anyone should take lightly."

Dylan's eyes lost some of their luster as he put his menu down next to hers.

"I never married Taffie in the temple, Megan. I always knew it wouldn't be that kind of marriage. You're the only woman I want to go through eternity with."

Megan felt the sweat pop out on her forehead. He wasn't comprehending the situation at all. He obviously didn't want to.

"I'm so sorry. That must have broken Taffie's heart."

Dylan laughed harshly and signaled the waiter.

"Bring us salads and breadsticks, now."

The waiter left promptly after taking their drink orders, leaving them facing each other once again.

"Stop feeling sorry for her, Megan. It was because of her that we're not together right now. She's the one who has kept us apart all these years."

Megan smoothed the napkin in her lap, not wanting to look Dylan in the eyes anymore. She hated hurting people, but he was insisting.

"Dylan, Taffie is not the reason we're not married today. I'm the one to blame for that. Don't you see, Dylan? If I had trusted you at all, we would have three kids and a house out in the country by now. But I didn't. And what's more, even if you had really done all those things, someone who sincerely loved you would have stuck by you and forgiven you. I'll be honest with you, I had been praying my heart out to get an answer from Heavenly Father that you were the right one for me. But I never got any answer. So when Taffie told me all of those lies that morning, I was more than willing to believe her, because I saw that as an answer to my prayers. It never felt right to me. Remember after you got back from your mission, and I insisted on being engaged for an entire year? There was a reason for that. Yes, I wanted to graduate from BYU, but there was more to it. We weren't meant to be together, Dylan. Not for a minute and definitely not for an eternity."

Dylan looked away from her, out the window at the passing people. He was quiet for so long, Megan didn't know what to do. Was he ill?

"What do you say to a man who has wasted the past eight years of his life wishing for someone he can never have?"

Megan reached across the table and grasped Dylan's hand in hers and smiled.

"I say, better eight than a lifetime."

Dylan tried to smile, but failed, and grimaced instead. He squeezed Megan's hand one last time, then let go.

"I guess I have a lot of thinking to do. I hope you don't mind, but I think I'll just forego lunch. I'm just not very hungry anymore. Please stay and eat though. I would be upset if you felt you had to leave."

Megan remembered why she agreed to meet Dylan in the first place and had to jump up and grab the sleeve of his suit-coat as he began to walk away.

"Please don't go yet. I have some questions for you that I need answers to."

Dylan looked curiously at her, then sat down, crossing his arms.

"Taffie said some things last night that I would like you to clarify for me. She said that information about my father was going to come to light that would humble my whole family. Do you know what she meant by that?"

Dylan's mouth tightened into a hard line, transforming his face. He now looked like the man she was more familiar with.

"You weren't the only one looking for a quick escape, Megan. Your dad's side of the business had started to pick up in the last month before the wedding. He started having second thoughts about the merger. Of course he didn't bother telling my dad that when he took two hundred thousand dollars of good faith money. He never did give it back, Megan. Your dad is a thief. A thief who's going to jail if we have anything to say about it. And we're not the only one's he's swindled. We're going to testify against him in court. Don't take it personally, Megan. This has nothing to do with you."

Megan raised shaky hands to her cheeks as she tried to take in everything Dylan had just dumped on her. Her own father? How could he do something like that?

"But he said the merger didn't happen because of me. He said that I'm the one who caused the disintegration of his business relationship with your father. He's blamed me for everything for the last eight years. He can barely even look me in the eye when he sees me, and when he does, he looks nauseated. He can't stand to be in the same room with me."

Dylan smiled sadly at Megan and got up from the table once again.

"You're just a reminder of his guilt. Nothing more."

Dylan turned and walked out of the restaurant and back to his life.

Chapter 23

As Megan watched Dylan disappear from sight, she realized she wasn't very hungry either. She wasn't sure what to do or what to think, but when she ended up in front of her mom and dad's house fifteen minutes later, she knew what needed to happen. She had to hear the truth from her father. Megan rang the doorbell five times before her mother finally answered the door.

"Megan, what on earth are you doing here, and why do you look like some kind of refugee?"

Megan ignored her mother's automatic verbal slap and walked in without an invitation.

"Is Dad here? I really need to talk to him."

Trisha shut the door and walked around Megan as if she smelled like something vile.

"He should be home anytime for lunch. We're playing tennis with the Wendells. I'm afraid he won't have time to talk to you today. Why don't you go home and get cleaned up and call him later tonight? We don't have any plans later, so he should be around."

Megan walked into the living room and sat down on one of the three black leather sofas arranged in a triangle.

"I'm not leaving until I talk to him, Mother. Do you think the Wendells would mind if I came along? I haven't played in years, but I used to be pretty good. Remember all of those lessons you made Linette and I take?"

Trisha looked alarmed at her daughter's determination to stay put. Megan always put her husband in a bad mood and she just couldn't handle his vicious temper today. Just the thought of another blow-up had her feeling frantic. She had to do something, so she went on the offensive. She couldn't push Megan out the door physically, but when it came to verbal pushing she was a heavy-weight champion.

"Speaking of Linette, when you're through brainwashing her, please feel free to send her home where she belongs. I think you two have had your fun long enough."

Megan felt her already strained stomach tighten further. Her mom had pulled out her claws and she knew how to draw blood. Megan had the scars to prove it.

"What exactly do you mean by brainwashing?" Megan asked softly.

Trisha smiled and knew automatically she had scored.

"You're a complete fanatic, Megan, admit it. Ever since you started going to church every Sunday, you've become some pathetic pale excuse for a person. You haven't seriously dated since Dylan and we know how wonderful that turned out. All you do is stay home, read your scriptures, and listen to your dog bark. For heaven's sakes just look at you! You don't even wear makeup anymore. You are a lifeless little robot and you're determined to make your sister into an exact replica of yourself. Trust me, one boring Molly Mormon is enough for this family."

Megan felt her chest constrict as pain filled her whole soul. How could a mother feel this way about her own daughter? Megan tried to remind herself that it was her mother who had the problem, but the pain clouded out her reasoning. It was just too much.

"Do you even have a heart beating in your chest, Mother? Did you ever love me?"

Trisha frowned as she walked over to her grand piano and whisked her fingers across the keys carelessly. "Don't be tedious, Megan. Just tell Linette that I'm giving her two more days to get this out of her system, and then I'm cutting her completely off. No more money. Ever."

Megan leaned her pounding head back against the soft leather of the sofa and buried her dreams of a reconciliation with her parents for good.

"Why do you want her back so badly? Oh, I get it, it's just you and Dad now. The pressure gets to you after a while, huh. Let's see, who's left to make Dad proud? You? It's almost like your life is one big beauty pageant, isn't it? I finally walked off the stage and Linette practically killed herself to get off. Did you even care that your daughter was anorexic? She could have died."

Trisha turned around to face her daughter, caught off guard by someone fighting back. She wasn't used to defending herself against her daughters. She'd never had to.

"She's naturally slender. She isn't anorexic. This is just another example of your deranged mind. Do you just sit around all day and make these fairy tales up? You really need to get a life before it's too late. I would hate to have you committed, although the idea is starting to grow on me."

Megan got to her feet slowly and walked over to the wall by the front window. The family portrait they'd had taken right before she had left for college hung in a prominent position, as if to show all of her parents' guests that they were a normal happy family. What a joke.

"I admit I do like fairy tales. I've always been fond of happy endings. Are you planning on a happy ending, Mom? How happy are you going to be when Dad's in jail for embezzlement or whatever they're charging him with, and you're stuck in this huge house all by yourself? No husband to pay your bills and no daughters to demean. That sounds like a tragedy to me."

Trisha sat down on the piano bench shakily. "What are you blabbering about, Megan? I want you to leave now. And don't come back. After I tell your father what you just said, I'm sure he'll disown you."

Megan heard her father's car drive up into the driveway and straightened her shoulders. After getting the truth from her father, there would be no reason to ever return. She was amazed at the feeling of relief that realization gave her.

"You better go get changed for tennis, Mom. You don't want to keep the Wendells waiting."

Trisha's eyes widened as she glanced at her watch. She wanted to impress the Wendells, and being late wasn't good for her image.

"You know where the door is. Use it," Trisha said.

Megan kept her back to her mom as Trisha practically ran from the room and up the stairs. She would have at least ten minutes alone with her dad. That's all it should take. She winced as the front door swung open.

"Trish, get a move on! I'll change at the club."

Megan walked into the entryway and leaned up against the wall with her arms crossed.

"She'll be about ten minutes, Dad. So while you're waiting, do you mind telling me why you stole two hundred thousand dollars from the Carlisles?"

Lane Garrett turned his head quickly to face his eldest daughter. His face looked haggard and strained as if he had been under a lot of pressure lately. He didn't look healthy at all.

"Why shouldn't I take the money? They owed me. What's it to you anyway? I'd think you'd be thrilled to see me stick it to the Carlisles after what Dylan pulled on you."

Megan flinched at the bitterness and ugliness emanating from her father. When had he become so twisted and mean? Growing up, she remembered him being distant and critical, but this was different. This was wrong.

"Give back the money, Dad, or you'll end up in jail. Do it for Mom's sake. Who will take care of her when you're in prison? Think of something else besides money for once."

Her father smiled acidly at Megan and jingled the change in

his pockets. Megan suddenly felt as if she needed to run, to get away from this house as fast as she could.

"I'm sure your mother's new boyfriend will take care of all of her wants and needs if I have to take some time off. I'm not worried, though. They can't touch me. My lawyer assures me I'm clean. The Carlisles are dreaming if they think they'll get one cent back. Oh, and by the way, I used some of that two hundred grand to pay for your college education. You might even want to send them a thank you," he said, laughing at his daughter's horrified expression.

Megan dashed around her father and out the door, wishing she could erase the sound of her father's cold laughter from her mind. Had she really come from those two people? Was it even possible for something good to come from something clearly so bad? Would she someday end up like them? The possibility made her nauseous as she drove quickly out of the elite subdivision and towards her humble home.

Chapter 24

Megan drove straight home and stumbled inside, numbly walking to her room where she fell face first onto her bed. She had been exhausted by Dylan and mercilessly drained by her parents. She didn't think she'd be able to move for the next three days. The only thing she had the energy to do was cry.

Her mind swelled up in waves of jumbled emotions. Anger, disbelief and jealousy. Why? Why had Trevor been born to Cora? Someone who would go to ridiculous lengths to make sure their child was happy. On the other hand, why had she been born to her parents? She knew there was an answer somewhere, she just wasn't sure she would like it.

Megan rolled onto her back and stared at the ceiling. If she continued to lay where she was, the likelihood of getting up the rest of the day would be nil. It was now or never. Megan commanded her body to move and headed for the bathroom. She wished a steaming hot shower could wash the slime by association feeling away. At the very least it would wake her up and hopefully rejuvenate her.

Megan was halfway through soaping her hair when the doorbell cut through the sound of water.

Oh no.

Megan rinsed quickly and grabbed for a towel, wrapping as she ran. It was too early for Trevor to be showing up, who in the world could she be expecting? Megan whipped the door open.

"Hi! We're here for our hair and makeup lesson."

Megan stared at the three Jarvis girls and mentally kicked herself in the behind. She needed a brain transplant operation, now. How could she have forgotten something as important as this?! And where was Linette when she needed her?

"Hey girls, come on in. Let me just grab some clothes and I'll be with you in just a minute."

The three girls walked into the front room, giggling and smiling nervously. They were obviously excited about the opportunity to play around with make-up, and Megan wanted this to be a fun experience for them. Why hadn't she planned ahead? Megan grabbed her brand new cell phone and ran back to her bedroom as she speed dialed Cora's phone number.

"Hello?"

"Hi, Cora. It's Megan. I was wondering if you had anything planned for this evening?"

"Well, not exactly. There's a good show coming on at seven that I wanted to see, but other than that, no. Why? Did you have something in mind?" Cora asked hopefully.

"What would you say if I invited you over for a few lessons on hair and makeup? I've got Drew's girls over here rearing to go, and I think I'm on shaky ground. I could really use some help with these make-overs."

Cora laughed, her eyes lighting up. She had been wanting to meet Drew's daughters and this would be the perfect opportunity. The girls would be meeting her as a friend of Megan's instead of their Dad's new romantic interest. She was already grabbing her purse as she answered Megan.

"I'll be there in less than twenty minutes. Just get their hair pulled back and their faces washed. This will be a piece of cake."

Megan put the phone down, smiling for the first time in hours. Her house was full of giggling girls and Cora would be there soon. It would be impossible to be sad under these circumstances. Maybe Heavenly Father was watching out for her after all.

* * *

"Am I having a bad dream, or did I just step into *Seventeen* magazine?"

Trevor put the flowers he had brought for Megan down on the coffee table and slipped out of his suit coat as he grinned at his mom and Megan, up to their eyeballs in curling irons, blush brushes, and fingernail polish.

"Trevor, you have perfect timing! I love that in a boyfriend. Would you mind coming over here and holding this section of hair for me? Your mom's all tied up and this has to look perfect."

Trevor's smile faltered slightly as he took hold of the section of hair Megan handed to him. It looked as if she were trying to recreate an African wedding ceremonial hairdo. He couldn't even count all of the loops of braids sticking out from the poor girl's head, but by the way the girl's eyes were shining, she was in heaven. Trevor's smile slipped back firmly into place as he watched the two most important women in his life primp three of the happiest girls to death.

"Ta da! What do you think, Trev? Aren't these three of the most beautiful girls you have ever seen? I think they look like models. What do you say?" Cora asked.

Trevor laughed at the look of triumph on his mother's face and knew his mom was just as happy as the girls were. She loved to be needed and helping these girls out with their make-overs had given her a beautiful glow. She looked as if she had been given a make-over.

"I'm almost positive that the five most beautiful women ever created are standing right here before me. I am humbled to be in your presence."

The three girls giggled and blushed at the compliments. It had to be true if it came from somebody as good looking as Megan's boyfriend.

"Well, all dressed up and nowhere to go? That's a real bummer. Do you girls think you're up to going to the food court at the mall? I'm starving to death," Trevor said.

The girls' eyes turned big and round with wonder. This was

almost too much. Most of the kids from school hung out at the mall, and if even one guy they knew could just see how stylish they really were, their lives would be complete.

Megan chuckled as she walked over to Trevor and kissed him firmly on the cheek, causing his eyebrows to shoot up into the air.

"You really do know how to make a girl's dreams come true, don't you?"

Trevor grinned and slid his arms around her waist, not caring if his mom and three teenage girls were watching and leaned down for a quick kiss.

"You think the food court is good, wait and see what I have in store for you."

Megan could feel herself blush and moved out of the circle of Trevor's arms smoothly. Trevor would just have to wait.

Chapter 25

After a quick trip to the mall for Chinese food, Cora dropped Megan and Trevor off at Megan's house while she took the girls home to their dad. Megan smiled to herself as she walked through the front door and threw her purse on the counter. How could such an awful day turn out to be so wonderful?

"What are you smiling about? You look like you know a secret."

Megan laughed, flopping tiredly down on her couch as she smiled up at Trevor who was now standing over her with his hands resting on his hips. Why was it he always reminded her of an eighth grader?

"I just think life can be so funny sometimes. Take your mom for instance. I think it's so sweet that the matchmaker is the one who got matched up. Did you notice how she insisted on taking the girls home? I think she wants to see Drew again. As a matter of fact, I think your mom is very interested in him. How do you feel about that?"

Trevor looked as if he suddenly didn't want to know her secret after all. He slouched down on the couch beside her, carelessly draping his arm around her shoulders.

"Well, to be honest, I don't like it."

Megan shrugged his arm from off her shoulders and turned to glare at him.

"Hey! Now don't look at me like that. Try and see it from my point of view. I've had my mom to myself ever since I was born. I've never even seen her look at another man. It's just kind of weird for me to see my mom dating. Have some compassion."

Megan relaxed back against the couch again, stiffening when his arm made its way back around her shoulders.

"Well, I think you should be supportive of her. I think it's wonderful and so romantic for her to find love after being alone for almost thirty years. And think of the cute stepsisters you'll have if your mom decides to marry Drew. Three sisters and two little brothers. Now that's a beautiful thought."

Megan snickered at Trevor's arrested look. He looked shocked by the thought of having so many sisters all at once. Poor thing. Poor Blaine! Blaine would most likely have to do all of the Christmas shopping.

"Make that four sisters. You forgot to count Linette," Trevor said too sweetly.

Megan's snickers stopped immediately as she turned to stare at Trevor.

"Trevor, I hope this isn't your way of proposing to me, because it's pretty off the wall, even for you."

Trevor grabbed the remote control from off of the coffee table and quickly turned on the TV.

"What channel was that English romance on anyway?"

Megan grabbed the remote from his hands, hiding it behind a throw pillow.

"Don't change the subject. You need to deal with this romance, right here. Are you seriously thinking about marriage?"

Trevor felt the familiar weight of the engagement ring in his pocket and wondered if he should spring it on her tonight. He looked at her from under half-closed lids and decided against it. He'd wait another week. But it couldn't hurt to have her start thinking in that direction.

"And what if I was? Haven't you thought of children and becoming a mother? Would it be so bad to get married to someone like me? Just picture yourself doing makeovers for your own daughters. Of course they'd have black, curly hair, but wouldn't that be something you'd like to do someday?"

Megan tilted her head and thought about becoming a mother. Would she be like her own mother, or would she be more like Cora? She sighed and knew the answer to that would be entirely up to her.

"Yes, I would like to be a mother. Very much. It's the husband part I'm worried about."

Trevor sat up, turning his body so he could massage Megan's shoulders and back.

"You would love it. Think of it, a massage every night. I might even do the dishes too. I'd probably pick up my socks. And . . . I'd take Marjorie for a walk every night."

Megan laughed, relaxing under the gentle massage. Forget the socks, though. If he'd just take over Marjorie's walks, that in itself would send her running to the altar.

"And what would you get in return? A twenty-eight year old failed real estate agent, a loser of a dog trainer, and a known bomb at relationships. I just don't think you've thought this through very well. You really don't know what you're getting yourself into."

As Trevor's hands stilled on her back, she turned to look up into his eyes. He looked very serious and fierce. Uh oh.

"I don't let anyone put my girlfriend down. Even you. So as your punishment, you have to come up with ten nice things to say about yourself in under one minute, or I get to kiss you. Starting now."

Megan's mouth fell open in surprise. Was he serious? Holy Hannah. He was looking intently at his watch and smiling. She'd better hurry.

"I can't believe you're doing this! Oh, all right. Umm, I'm pretty good at budgeting money. I have great taste in houses. I'm a really good hair braider. I make the best lasagna in the world. Yes, even better than your mothers. Umm, I think my toes are cute. I'm really good at packing suitcases. I've never had any cavities. I'm a safe driver. I read my scriptures every day. And finally, I have great taste in English romances."

With that she grabbed the remote she had hidden under the pillow and flipped on the TV, turning it to A&E just in time to hear the opening score of Jane Austen's Pride and Prejudice. She laughed at Trevor's dramatic anguish and decided that it wouldn't be so bad after all to have his arm around her during the show. It might even be nice.

During a commercial, Trevor turned down the volume and tickled her ear to get her attention.

"So how was your date with Dylan? Did he propose to you? I bet he offered you children with ordinary straight, blond hair."

Megan grimaced and stretched before answering. She didn't really want to go into everything that had happened. She didn't want to see her good mood disappear.

"Well, put your mind at rest. Dylan has accepted the fact that I am not interested in pursuing a relationship with him at this time. Or any time for that matter. So you see, everything is just the way it should be."

Trevor looked into her eyes searchingly, as if he were trying to read her mind.

"You know, you can talk to me about anything. You do know that don't you? Anything at all."

Megan winced at the memory of being with her parents that afternoon and knew she didn't want him to know how dysfunctional her family really was. He'd reconsider that cubic zirconium.

"Oh, Trevor. Do you really want to be disillusioned this early in our relationship?"

Trevor frowned thoughtfully and then looked Megan straight in the eye. "Megan, if there is something that is upsetting you, then I want to know what it is. When you care about someone, then you have a natural urge to make everything better. To help. Please, disillusion me."

Megan groaned as she massaged her temples. She really didn't want to tell Trevor that her father was a thief. Call her a coward, but she did have her pride. She'd just have to walk around the truth a little bit.

"What do you do when someone hurts you badly. What do you do when you have all of these feelings of pain and anger and you don't know what to do with them. I feel like I'm going to be swallowed up by it all. It's like my mind is in constant replay of every bad thing they've ever done or said to me and I just can't get over it. I went over to my parents' house after my lunch with Dylan and we had a major confrontation. I wanted to deal with a couple issues and they flat out didn't. My mom pretty much disowned me and my dad couldn't help laughing as I walked out the door. It wasn't a very pleasant afternoon."

Trevor sighed and grabbed on to Megan's hand, squeezing it comfortingly. "Oh Megan, I'm so sorry. It looks like you have a pretty big task ahead of you."

Megan blinked, caught off guard. That wasn't exactly what she had expected to hear. "What do you mean by that?"

Trevor leaned his head back against the couch and closed his eyes for a moment as he tried to put what was in his heart, into words.

"You have a big weight just sitting on your spirit. Right?"

Megan nodded her head in agreement. That was pretty much it in a nut shell.

"The only way to get rid of that weight is to forgive your parents. You have to forgive them of everything."

Megan sat up in surprise. "Didn't you hear anything I just said. You wouldn't even believe me if I told you what they've done! It's so easy for you to sit there and say forgive them. You were raised by Cora the Great. She was the perfect mom. You probably don't even realize that there are moms and dads out there who really don't care about their kids. There are some emotionally and physically abused people out there, and all they have to do is forgive? Are you kidding me?"

Trevor grabbed Megan's shoulders and pulled her back to sit beside him. He put his arms around her, holding her gently, and then surprised her again.

"No. I don't kid around about the Atonement. You're right, though. I was raised by a wonderful woman who was completely unselfish. But that doesn't mean I haven't had to deal with my share of anger and hurt and pain. No one, regardless of what kind of parents they have, is immune to suffering."

Megan looked at him doubtfully, not wanting to believe that all she had to do was to simply forgive her parents. As if that would take away all the pain she was feeling. Trevor reached in his pocket for his wallet and pulled out a ragged piece of paper that looked as if it were a hundred years old. He smoothed it out almost reverently and then looked at her expectantly, as if he were about to say something earth shattering.

"What?" She asked, starting to feel irritated.

"My mom doesn't even know this, but when I was on my mission in Guatemala, my companion and I were attacked from behind. There was about five of them, and they beat us up pretty bad. My companion had to go to the hospital and get stitches. They gave me two black eyes, a broken nose, and this scar on my chin. I don't even think it was because we were missionaries. I think it was because they were just bored and wanted to have some fun. A week after the beating, we were at a zone conference, and one of the sister missionaries came up to me and handed me this quote. It's from Ann Madsen. The sister had heard her give a talk at a women's conference and she wrote it down. It really helped me. Do you want to hear it?"

Megan shrugged her shoulders casually. She'd listen to anything if it made her feel better.

"'Forgiveness is one of our tasks, as we partake of the sacrament. If we would be forgiven, we must, ourselves, forgive. To truly forgive, I must identify the hurt, the pain—honestly, not denying it—and then offer that pain as a willing sacrifice to God. Then it can disappear. Once I've given it away, my attitude toward the person who inflicted it is also changed; no grievance or wound remains, and he or she can be seen in a new light. The other person need do nothing for this to happen. It is in my heart that the 'mighty change' can take place.'"

Megan relaxed slightly as she thought about what Trevor had just said. It was possible he had a point. But she needed a little more time to think about it. Praying about it probably wouldn't hurt either.

"Thanks," was all she said and gave Trevor a hug. He traced her eyebrows with his forefinger, causing goosebumps to rise up on her arms. It was only natural that Megan lean up and kiss him gently on the lips. Trevor's surprised grin had her wondering if maybe she should be curbing those natural instincts.

"Umm, I forgot to thank you for the phone and the credit card. That was very thoughtful of you. But I'm surprised you haven't called me on it yet. I know you have my number."

Trevor knew he was being put off, but didn't mind. The night was still young.

"Hmm, yes, but I have been very busy lately. Moving a business compound is harder than it sounds. But after that's all done, I'll have much more time to devote to you. And that's the reason for the credit card. You can be busy having fun and shopping in the meantime. What have you bought with it so far? I wouldn't mind a little fashion show."

Trevor knew darn well she hadn't bought a stick of gum with it, which fact irked him greatly. He was very curious at her resistance.

Megan's mouth quirked up as she wondered what to tell him. Should she tell him the truth that she thought he was insane if he thought he could buy her affections, or should she be a little more diplomatic?

"Well, I guess I just can't make up my mind what to buy first. I'm trying to decide between a beach house in the Caribbean or a ski lodge at Sundance. What do you think?"

Trevor's eyes widened in surprise. *Wow!* He had really misjudged her. Then he saw her mouth twitch and the twinkle in her eyes and knew she was making fun of him. He grabbed her and tickled her until she squealed for mercy.

"You little brat! You really had me going there for a while."

Megan held her stomach as she continued to laugh at the horrified expression she had seen bloom on his face. He was turning out to be a lot of fun to tease.

"What are you thinking, giving me a credit card? Why don't we stick with flowers and candy?"

Trevor growled at her and reached over to tickle her again but she was ready this time and jumped over onto the love seat, keeping a safe distance between them.

"Flowers and candy get a little boring after a while and think of all the time you're saving Blaine by picking out your own gifts. You'd be doing him a big favor."

Megan rolled her eyes and then rolled onto her stomach, with her feet waving in the air. She looked just like a teenager. Trevor couldn't stop from smiling at her.

"Well, if you put it that way. Why don't you give me some ideas of what you expect me to buy with it? I'm a little new at this sort of thing."

Trevor let out a huge sigh of relief. Now they were getting down to business.

"That's easy enough. You can buy yourself anything really. I would wait on the ski lodges and beach houses until our relationship becomes a tad more formal, but other than that, your limits are what you make them. Let's see, you could buy your new boyfriend a tie, or Marjorie a new leash, that sort of thing, or you could get more adventurous and say, get yourself a new car. Or, if you want to quit your job and go back to school for your masters degree, that would be up to you."

Megan asked just out of curiosity. "I hope this isn't a rude question, but what exactly is the credit limit on my card?"

Trevor studied her for a minute before answering. What was going on inside her head? She looked as if she were asking just to make him feel better.

"That specific card has a five hundred thousand dollar limit, with an option for a two hundred and fifty thousand dollar cash advance."

Megan smiled slowly then went over and sat down next to Trevor again on the couch, grabbing his arm and pulling it around her shoulders.

"Trevor, that's a lot of faith to have in somebody. Have I told you lately that you're the best boyfriend I've ever had?"

Trevor looked down at her suspiciously and shook his head. She had caved in a lot quicker than he had bargained for. He would just have the credit card company notify him immediately the moment she used the card. He wouldn't be able to relax until he knew what was brewing in her mind.

The front door flew open as Linette and Blaine breezed in, laughing and giggling together like little kids.

Trevor scowled, knowing his plans for kissing Megan had just gone up in smoke. He'd be lucky to get a good night hug now. Rotten Blaine! To Trevor's horror, they all stayed up watching the first part of Pride and Prejudice, then he and Blaine were kicked out the door at ten o'clock sharp. Trevor shook his head in frustration as he got in his car to drive home. Besides the fact that he hadn't been properly kissed goodnight, things were coming along rather well. He wasn't sure what to think of her parents, but Megan seemed like she really wanted to work through it. She impressed him more each day. And if he could just keep her on schedule, then he wouldn't have to change their flight plans to Venice. But, if he had to push the wedding back a couple of days then he could deal with that. Or rather, Blaine would. He was so good at working out the details.

Chapter 26

The next week was a blur of lunch dates, candle light dinners and long walks. Everything she'd always wanted. A little romance. Dylan's idea of romance had always been either watching sports on TV together or going to parties. Always a lot of noise and excitement, but not a lot of intimacy. Who'd have thought that Trevor, the seminary president, had it in him? Megan smiled as she did her laundry. Linette was supposed to meet her at home for lunch and then they were going to get ready for their dates that night. Trevor and Blaine had planned a big double date together, and were keeping it a surprise. Megan shook her head in wonder. Her life was so different now compared to a month ago. It was amazing what a little love could do for someone.

Wait a second. Megan dropped a shirt and put both hands over her mouth. Had she really fallen in love with Trevor Riley? Megan left the laundry room and walked aimlessly towards the kitchen. She sat on one of her bar stools at the counter and rested her head in her arms. Maybe she wasn't such a bomb at relationships after all? Maybe this had a chance of working. Megan blinked, realizing she had just fallen in love with a very wealthy man. Would it be okay to take his money now that she knew she loved him? He would give her anything she wanted. Megan looked over at the credit card laying on the counter and knew exactly what she wanted. A week ago when Trevor had told her what her credit limit was, the idea had popped into her head immediately, but she had hesitated. She could never take advantage of a boyfriend to that extent, even if he was practically begging her to. On the other hand, taking advantage of a fianceé was perfectly natural. And very acceptable. She picked up the card looking it over thoughtfully. It could wait until Monday though. She had a date tonight and she wanted plenty of time to get ready. Megan walked over to her purse and put the card in her wallet.

* * *

Blaine and Trevor showed up at four o'clock sharp, dressed in jeans and t-shirts. Megan and Linette looked at each other in dismay. There had been a major miscommunication as far as what a "big" date constituted.

"Uh, sweetie? I thought you said tonight was going to be the best date we've ever been on? Umm, . . . either you're a little casual, or we're very overdressed," Megan said, looking down at her high heels, silk skirt and wrap-around silk shirt. Linette was even worse. She was wearing sequins. Megan started to snicker at Linette's expression. She was horrified.

"No problem, just hurry and throw on a pair of old jeans and a T-shirt. We've got ten minutes. No rush," Trevor said as he stared at his watch grimly.

Blaine was busy changing the time on his watch and didn't seem to realize there was even a mix-up. Megan and Linette exchanged bleak expressions and then turned and ran into their rooms. Megan took the clip out of her hair, pulling off her clothes in seconds. She rummaged through her closet for her raggediest pair of jeans and pulled an old Hard Rock Cafe T-shirt out of her dresser drawer. She should have known. A guy's idea of the perfect date had nothing to do with dressing up. What had she been thinking? She pulled on a pair of running shoes and grabbed a rubber band to pull her hair back into a pony tail. She glanced into her dresser mirror and frowned. What had taken two hours to create had been destroyed in under two minutes. This had better be worth it.

She joined Linette and the guys in the living room, and was quickly hustled outside and practically pushed into the car. Trevor was driving, and the way he was swerving in and out of traffic, had her wondering if pretending to be a race car driver was part of this fantasy date. Megan shook her head in exasperation. Next date, she was planning.

Fifteen minutes later they arrived at the mini-airport in Provo, where a helicopter was waiting for them. Megan and Linette gaped at each other, not wanting to admit to their dates that both of them were afraid of flying. They were pulled inside quickly, before they even had a chance to run for it. This was getting worse by the second. Megan kept her eyes closed the entire time, holding onto Trevor's hand in a death grip and hiding her head in his shoulder. She thought she heard gagging sounds at one point, but didn't dare peek to see if Linette was okay. She was on her own.

As she felt the helicopter touch down, a huge sense of relief swept over her, making her supremely thankful to be alive. She opened her eyes cautiously and looked for Linette first. Her sister was alive but very green. Megan rubbed her arms briskly to get the circulation going again, and then followed Trevor off the helicopter. What in the world were they in for now?

The pilot threw Blaine and Trevor two large, heavy-looking back packs and saluted before taking off again. Trevor and Blaine put the packs on and then smiled at their dates expectantly.

"Isn't this great?" Blaine asked Linette with a boyish grin.

Linette turned around and threw up in a bush.

After giving Linette a few minutes to recuperate, they were off. Megan focused on her surroundings, and realized that they were practically on top of a mountain. Which mountain, she had no idea. She'd never been big on hiking. One look at Trevor's exuberant face though, and she knew automatically, he was in his element.

"Come on, girls. It's just over this little ridge and then we'll be there. Blaine didn't think you'd want to hike the whole thing, so you can blame him for the helicopter ride. Just wait, you'll love it."

Megan watched as Blaine and Trevor practically ran up the mountain. She took her sister's hand in hers and pulled and dragged her two miles up and over the teeny little ridge. Trevor was really going to have to pay for this.

"Megan, if I ever go out with Blaine again, please feel free to have my brain examined."

Megan sighed, knowing that it wasn't just Blaine. All men had their ideas of what a perfect date was. Now, just to get through the night.

"Come on, slow pokes! I thought you two were in shape. We've already got camp set up," Blaine called to them.

Megan looked for the nearest rock to throw. Camp? They'd set up camp? Surely they didn't expect them to camp. Surely. Megan and Linette hobbled the last few yards to their "camp-site." Cute. Really cute. A large blanket thrown on the ground.

Blaine and Trevor had made a fire and were in the process of roasting hot dogs. Now it was her turn to throw up in the bushes. Linette couldn't hold back a groan and the smile Megan gave Trevor wasn't exactly the brightest, but they walked the rest of the way and sat down on the hard, rocky ground next to their dates.

"Hot dogs. Yummy. Is there a beverage to go along with the main course?"

Trevor grinned at Megan and threw her a canteen. Megan looked at it cautiously but undid the lid and took a swig. Yep, just as she thought. Water that tasted exactly like a canteen. Megan was actually really proud of Linette when she ate half of her hot dog. For someone fighting anorexia, that was huge. She could only manage half herself before chucking it into the bushes behind them. For dessert, they roasted marshmallows. Megan couldn't help smiling at Trevor and Blaine. They were so proud of themselves, they could barely sit still.

Megan leaned over and whispered into Linette's ear, "Do

you ever get the feeling that we're dating Tom Sawyer and Huckleberry Finn?" Linette laughed softly, but shook her head. "You mean, two wannabes, right? I bet you the last time these two were this close to a mountain was at scout camp when they were sixteen."

Megan looked over to where Blaine and Trevor were studying some kind of animal print in the dirt, and knew Linette was probably right. But they were in heaven, so she let them stay there.

Watching the sunset made everything worth it. Even the hot dog. It was incredible. The oranges, blues and purples went beyond visual sensation. Feeling nature surround you, while seeing something not even Monet could get right was a price-less gift. Maybe Trevor hadn't screwed up as bad as she had thought.

The two couples laid down on the blankets, resting their heads on their hands and counted the stars. Megan wasn't even surprised when she heard Linette whisper to Blaine, "This is the best date I've ever been on." Megan laughed out loud when she heard Blaine's reply, "I know."

Megan looked over at Trevor and realized that this was the first time she had seen him totally and completely relaxed. He looked good. The sharp planes of his face had softened in the disappearing sunlight, and there was a faint smile on his face. Megan couldn't help reaching over and whispering in his ear.

"You win. It only took a few weeks, but I like you very, very much, Trevor."

Trevor raised one eyebrow suspiciously as he tore his eyes away from the sunset to gaze at Megan with his dark eyes.

"'Like' is such a bland little word, isn't it? Are you sure you wouldn't want to change it to something a little more passionate?"

Megan smiled, not saying a word, as she snuggled closer to Trevor on the blanket. He could wait.

Chapter 27

"Hurry up, Linette! We're going to be late for church."
Megan yelled behind her as she walked outside to say hello to
Marjorie. Her foot knocked into a box that had been shoved to
the side of the door. Megan grinned, wondering what Trevor
was up to now. He never quit. Megan tore the packing tape off
the box and reached in and grabbed a book. Megan frowned as
she opened the cover and one of her baby pictures fell out. This
was not from Trevor. This was from her parents. They had
dumped off all of her scrapbooks and baby pictures. They obviously had no use for them anymore. Megan felt her heart seize
and almost quit. She dropped her head to rest on the book in
her hands and felt the tears run down her wrists. Her parents
had wanted to send her a message and this one was loud and
clear. Megan hoped that Linette wouldn't walk out and find
their parent's little surprise. Megan noticed a smaller box to the
side and knew automatically they were her sister's pictures.
Her parents were nothing if not thorough. Megan hefted the
boxes into the garage, deciding to deal with it after church. She
didn't want to upset Linette. She was doing so well with her
counseling and her eating habits, that she didn't want to risk a
relapse. Linette had gained five pounds. Five fabulous pounds
that she wasn't going to see her parents whittle away again.

"What are you doing, Meg? Let's go, I'm ready."

Megan pulled an old blanket over the boxes and then joined
her sister on the sidewalk. The walk to church would help to
cool down her emotions. What she really needed was a bucket
of ice.

Linette and Megan found a seat towards the back of the

chapel and sat down just as the prelude music ended. Megan studied Linette carefully from the corner of her eyes. She knew from experience that Linette had very little in religious background, but Megan could sense that Linette was happy to be here. She was smiling and holding her scriptures on her lap, just ready to turn the pages as soon as someone announced a chapter and verse. Sometimes it took so little to kill a person's spiritual hunger, and at other times, it didn't matter what one's life was—nothing could kill that hunger. Linette was strong, and with the Spirit in her life, she would be on the right path. Now, just to make sure she was on the right one herself.

During the sacrament, Megan thought about the quote Trevor had read to her. Was it possible to be the exception when it came to forgiveness? Did Heavenly Father really expect her to forgive her mom and dad, especially after the stunt they pulled just that morning? Megan shook her head in frustration, but as she took the bread in her hand, she knew she wasn't the exception. No one was. When the deacons passed the water, she hesitated, but she drank hoping it would give her the strength to even make an attempt.

Megan sat back and decided to really listen to the talks today, not zone them out as she sometimes did when she had a lot on her mind. She'd rather think of anything besides her problems. There was no point in depressing herself. She smiled as Sister Lyman made her way to the stand. She was at least seventy, but she was a ball of fire. If there was anyone who needed help in the ward, she was the first one in line with a casserole or card. Megan had always felt very comfortable around her. Almost loved. She would do her best to listen to every word that came out of her mouth.

"Brothers and sisters, the bishop has asked that I speak to you today on forgiveness."

Megan's mouth fell open. This couldn't be a coincidence. She didn't believe in them. Heavenly Father was really trying to make his point. Megan rubbed her hands over her face and reminded herself to listen. If Heavenly Father had gone to all this trouble for her, then she'd better do her part and be open to it. Who knew? Maybe Sister Lyman would give the other side of forgiveness, if there was one. Or was that called bitterness? Maybe she would be let off the hook? Megan frowned, knowing she was grabbing at straws, but wishing with all her heart that she didn't have to deal with this.

"From Dennis Rasmussen's book, *The Lord's Question*, we read, 'Evil multiplies by the response it seeks to provoke, and when I return evil for evil, I engender corruption myself. The chain of evil is broken for good when a pure and loving heart absorbs a hurt and forbears to hurt in return. . . . Deep within every child of God, the Light of Christ resides, guiding, comforting, purifying the heart that turns to him.'"

Megan reached over to Linette and said something about using the ladies room, and left as fast as she could. She walked outside and leaned against a maple tree that was at least a hundred years old and let her breath out. Why was this happening to her? Why would God give her a task, when he knew it was impossible? What good could come of her failure to accomplish this? Megan closed her eyes tightly and prayed. She prayed for the desire to forgive. She didn't pray to forgive; she settled for just the wanting of it. As she pleaded with Heavenly Father, right there in front of the church, the funniest thing started to happen to her. She started to feel good. No, it was happy. She started to feel happy. Megan ended her prayer and knew that Heavenly Father, in his own way, had just given her a hug. He had leaned down from heaven and wrapped his arms around her, making all the bad feelings go away, if only for a moment. Just to show her that he could. It really was possible.

Megan walked back inside the church, flicking the tears from her cheeks and smiled in relief. Heavenly Father hadn't given her an impossible task. It was just a simple task. A decision. It was up to her, yes or no. As she passed a picture of Jesus kneeling in Gethsemane, she knew her answer was yes. She would do it for Him.

Chapter 28

Megan woke up the next morning, more energized and excited than she had been in years. She had a mission. Megan had floor time that morning, but what she needed to do would only take a few minutes. Just enough time to conquer the world, and make it over to the jewelers to pick out a ring for Trevor. She had prayed about it the night before and whether Trevor was being serious or not, she and the Lord had decided, he was the man for her.

She couldn't stop smiling at the thought of having black, curly-haired children, and chuckled at the image of Cora being the world's greatest grandmother. And Trevor. She tried to think of the exact moment she had fallen in love with him and decided it had to have been in high school, when she had seen him walk from the seminary building to their high school. That had been the day she had fought with her parents over signing up for seminary. What was that saying? Good things come to those who wait. Well, she had waited long enough and Trevor was very good.

Megan "outfloated" Linette that morning, making her sister giggle and point her finger at her.

"Shouldn't you be giggling your way to school?" Megan asked.

Linette grabbed her books and opened the door before retorting, "Don't you think you should be seeing other people? Aren't you going a little fast, Meg? I wouldn't want you to get hurt or anything."

Megan groaned and then laughed anyway. "That bad, huh?

Okay, I'll do the dishes tonight to make up for being such a typical older sister."

Linette poked her head back into the door with a grin on her face. "It feels good, doesn't it?"

Megan nodded her head in complete agreement. Being in love was the best feeling in the world.

Chapter 29

Trevor hung up the phone and turned slowly around in his sleek black leather chair to stare out the window of his make-shift office. He was having a brand new office complex built in Lehi, overlooking the golf course at Thanksgiving Point. But until then, he was making do in a small, cramped office building in Sandy.

He got up from his desk and leaned his head against the cool window pane. How could the spirit be so wrong? It was happening to him all over again. Why did he insist on having relationships with women who only wanted to use him for his money? He tried not to think about Saturday night, and how she had seemed so open to him. And from the way she had kissed him, he would have sworn she meant it. Trevor reached into his pants pocket and pulled out the small black box he had been carrying around for weeks as a good luck charm and opened it up. Megan was right; he should stick to cubic zirconium rings. He took the diamond out and felt his heart rip in two. He wished the emeralds didn't remind him so strongly of Megan's eyes. As far as he was concerned, his grandmother's ring should have stayed where it belonged. On his grandmother's hand. He turned and made a perfect three point shot into the waste paper basket and couldn't help thinking how beautifully it sparkled as it arced downward towards the remains of his lunch. He hoped the custodian would be by soon. He didn't want the reminder of his naivete anywhere near him. The nearest landfill would be the most suitable place for his innocence.

* * *

Megan smiled with delight as she left the jeweler's store with a gold wedding band in her purse. It was simple, but she knew it would suit Trevor perfectly. A wide band of gold was all he would need to know that he was hers. She had used up the rest of her commission check to pay for it. She laughed, making people turn and stare at her, as she wondered how Trevor was going to respond to having the tables turned on him. How would he react? He'd better jump up and shout yes; otherwise she would feel very silly. But from the way he had been acting, she knew he would be delighted with her. Now all she had to do was plan the scene. Where should it happen? She wanted it to be memorable so her grandkids would have something to sigh over. But where? And then the thought came to her. What better place to propose than at the temple? Now all she had to do was get him there. She knew he was busy, so she'd have to come up with a surefire way of getting his interest. Maybe a little mind game would do the trick. Megan pulled out her incredibly handy cell phone and the piece of paper that had Trevor's secret phone number on it. She giggled to herself helplessly as she dialed the number.

"Hello?"

"Trevor, it's Megan. Meet me at 742 North 900 East in American Fork, in one hour sharp. We have to talk."

Megan hung up the phone, not waiting for a reply. She'd bet her next mortgage payment he was fifteen minutes early. Megan ran to her car, already planning what her wedding announcements would say. Poor Trevor, was he in for a shock!

Chapter 30

Trevor put his cell phone down on the desk and ran his hands through his hair. What was she trying to pull? She had sounded so cold, as if she were mad at him. Then it dawned at him. This was her breakup scene. She had most likely planned it the moment she had heard he was a millionaire at the reunion. Should he let her have her moment, or should he leave her hanging? What would she do if he just never showed up? Or he could pull one over on her and break up with her before she even opened her mouth. But that would be so juvenile and he was very curious as to what her reason for dumping him would be. This would be his only chance to confront her. She had the guts to take two hundred thousand dollars of his money and transfer it straight into Carlisle and Beckstead Inc.'s bank account. He wanted to know if she had the guts to admit to him what she had done. Trevor took one last look at Megan's high school picture he'd had blown up and put in a sterling silver frame. He grabbed the picture off his desk and laid it gently on top of the diamond ring. Trevor walked quickly out the door. He didn't want to be late.

* * *

Megan paced up and down the walkway, glancing at her Timex every few seconds. She couldn't believe he was late! It was a good thing she hadn't seriously bet her mortgage payment—she would be in huge trouble. How was she going to explain to her grandkids that their grandfather had been obnoxiously late to his own proposal? Megan's shoulders slumped in relief as she saw his car pull into the parking lot.

Trevor usually walked with such vigor and energy, but

today he was walking so slowly, as if he were sick or exhausted. Maybe today wasn't the best day for her to propose to him? Nah, what better way to put a smile on his face. She took one last look up at the temple spires for courage and then walked the rest of the way to meet him.

"I'm guessing you took the long way."

Trevor didn't even crack a smile. Megan frowned. He must really be having a bad day. Well, she knew one way to make his day better.

"Well, since you're here, would you mind coming over here to sit down on this bench? I have a question for you."

Trevor's blood had turned to fire. He was so furious, he could barely contain himself from ringing her neck. How dare she tell him to take a hike on the sacred grounds of the temple? He should be relieved to find out how sick and depraved she was before he had offered her eternity. Trevor sat down and stared coldly up at Megan, who must be really charged up about taking his heart out and stomping it into the ground, because she looked really excited. Trevor was beginning to feel ill.

"Trevor, would you do me the great honor of marrying me?"

Megan pulled the ring she had slid onto her own finger and reached down for Trevor's cold and lifeless hand. She grinned at him as she slid the simple gold band onto his left hand. Perfect fit. Perfect husband for her.

"What?"

Megan looked irritated by his question, but restrained herself and tried one more time.

"I'm asking you to marry me. You know, in the temple, for eternity, that sort of thing. Don't tell me you need time to think about it?"

Megan looked unsure of herself as she stared down at Trevor's dumbfounded expression. If this turned out to be just one more humiliating experience for her, she was going to move to Alaska. Could she have read the signs so wrong? He had been coming on so strong. He had even talked about marriage just last week!

"What?"

Megan stomped her foot, yanked the ring off of his finger and walked stiffly away from the romantic setting towards her car. She would have just enough time to pack all of her clothes and catch a plane to Anchorage. She would find a nice dark cave, hopefully without a grizzly bear and hibernate for the rest of her life. What an idiot she had been!

Trevor watched Megan's quickly disappearing form and tried to understand the events of the last five minutes. He wouldn't be getting any answers from her if she took off, and a surge of new anger had Trevor on his feet and sprinting after Megan who was now unlocking her car door.

"How can you play with somebody's emotions like that? I am a person who breathes and feels and bleeds just like anybody else. Did you think I wouldn't find out about your little game? What were you going to do? Wait until after the wedding and then take me for millions? You got greedy, didn't you . . . or was it Dylan? Now that I'm thinking more clearly, this was all his plan, wasn't it? Then, after he's divorced and you're divorced you can both retire to your choice of Caribbean bungalow or love nest in the canyon. Heck, take both, you'll have enough money then, won't you?"

Megan's mouth went slack with shock. Did Trevor have a mental disorder Cora had never bothered to mention? What was he talking about? She was the one who was offended here! He had no right to look so . . . so completely devastated? Megan walked around the car and took Trevor's hand in hers. This time, it wasn't lifeless, it was balled up with pent-up rage and emotion.

"Trevor, look at me. Look at me. Whatever it is you think I've done, I haven't. Now, why don't we walk back to that little bench and sit down and you can tell me all about it."

Trevor didn't want to follow her back towards the temple, but when she had taken his hand and told him to look at her, she had seemed so sincere and genuine. Almost as if she was innocent. Well, fine. He would just confront her with her betrayal and watch her crumble with guilt.

"You transferred two hundred thousand dollars from your credit card account into Carlisle's bank account. Do you deny this?"

Megan looked surprised for a second and then smiled. Of all things.

"Nope. I don't. Remember, you said I could spend it on anything I wanted to."

Trevor groaned deep in his chest and got up from the bench for the last time. This was just too painful. He couldn't stand to see her smile as she admitted she had given Dylan his money. Forget her crumbling, he was about to disintegrate.

"Trevor, wait! My father stole two hundred thousand dollars from Dylan's father. That's what I found out when I had lunch with him. I went to talk to my dad about it, and he freely admitted it. He told me he used part of the money to pay for my college education. He even laughed about it. So when you told me the other day that I could go back to school, it gave me the idea. I just wanted to be completely free from the past. From Dylan and from my parents. I didn't want my children to have that kind of legacy. I didn't want your children to carry that burden. I'll pay you back when we're married. I'm sure I'll sell another house someday. I only get six percent commission, but it really adds up after a while. I'm sorry if I hurt you, but you said I could spend it on anything I wanted to."

Trevor turned slowly around to face a now very insecure and unhappy woman. If what she said was true, then . . .

Trevor grabbed Megan's hand and pulled her at a run towards his car, grinning and whooping as he worked the gold band out of her clenched fist and back onto his finger.

"Get in, sweetheart! We have to catch the custodian."

* * *

Megan leaned back into the tub filled with bubbles and held her left hand up to admire for the hundredth time. It had taken her twenty minutes to clean all of the pizza sauce out of the crevices, but it had been worth it. She still couldn't believe how furious she had been at Trevor when instead of explaining a few details to her, he said, "I'll explain later." He then chose to sing to his favorite James Brown CD, at the top of his lungs, all the way to his office building, completely ignoring her. He had horribly embarrassed her when he had dragged her laughing and jumping all the way up to his office on the top floor of the building complex. Everyone had stared at them as if they were lunatics. And as she witnessed him dumping his trash all over his immaculate office, she knew for sure she was changing her phone number. But she would always remember the shock and delight she had felt when he crammed the dirtiest ring she had ever seen onto her finger. It had been the most romantic moment of her life.

And then he had kissed her. Of all the kisses in her life, this one was it. The kiss of a lifetime. She had felt it from the top of her head to the tips of her toes. She now understood the theory of spontaneous combustion much better.

It was probably a good thing he'd had to catch a plane right then. Sometimes distance was a good way to make sure you were subscribing to all of the celestial dating laws.

Megan stuck her pruny toes out of the water and sighed with happiness. Men and women were that they might have joy. She would take her smidgen of it and be very thankful.

Chapter 31

Two weeks later, Megan found herself sitting between Linette and Cora on Cora's living room couch having a surprise bridal shower. Trevor hadn't been kidding around when he had called her the next day and told her that he wanted to get married soon. They were scheduled to be sealed in the Timpanogos Temple in American Fork on that coming Saturday morning. Every time she thought about it, she had to catch her breath. They were foregoing the reception and taking their close friends and family out to lunch at the Tree Room at Sundance instead. They would be catching a flight to Italy that same night.

"Megan, this is your bridal shower. It wouldn't hurt to pay attention."

Megan snapped back to her surroundings immediately, blushing as her sister laughed at her.

"Sorry, guys. I was just thinking about my honeymoon."

The whole room erupted into hysterical laughter, causing Megan to turn an even darker shade of red.

"I didn't mean it that way! Come on, I'm back on track now. Hand me that big present in the back. It's been calling out to me ever since I walked in the door."

Jackie jumped up and grabbed the present for Megan, handing it to her with a grin.

"You really had me fooled, Megan. I thought you and me would end up old maids together and here you are marrying the most eligible bachelor of the year. You have to promise to set me up with one of his friends."

Megan shook her head and laughed as she tore the wrapping paper off.

"As if you need any help."

Megan groaned and rolled her eyes as she pulled out yet another item of lingerie.

"Aren't I supposed to be getting toasters and towels? I can open up my very own Victoria's Secret store now."

Brenna grabbed the lingerie Megan was holding and checked the size and smiled.

"Tell you what. I'll trade you my toaster and a couple towels for this one."

Megan snatched the nightgown back, giggling as all of the women surrounding her started grabbing all of her gifts.

"I take it back! I love my presents! Hey, Linette, that one's my favorite. You have to wait for your own shower."

Linette whimpered pathetically as she handed her sister the cream satin pajamas back.

"Who knows when I'll have my own bridal shower? I think it's customary to actually be engaged first."

Megan gave her sister a quick hug.

"Not everyone moves as fast as Trevor does. Just give Blaine some time. After he sees how ecstatic Trevor is when he's married, you know Blaine will want to be just as happy. They have matching cars, for Pete's sake. Why not matching sisters, too?"

Linette sighed and slumped down on the couch next to Cora, who automatically put her arm around Linette's still thin shoulders. Megan smiled at the relationship the two women were developing. Cora was turning out to be the mother they both desperately needed and wanted.

"Hey everyone, don't eat all the hors d'oeuvres before I get back," Megan warned everyone, then walked down the hall to use the bathroom. All of the sparkling apple cider was finally getting to her. She tried the door, but it was locked. Brenna must have beaten her to it. Megan glared at the closed door and walked further down the hall towards Cora's bedroom. She was sure Cora wouldn't mind. After all, it was an emergency.

As she walked out of Cora's bathroom five minutes later, she paused as she saw a carelessly strewn contract on Cora's dresser. She was almost positive she had seen her name at a glance. It wasn't one of her real estate contracts either. Why would her name be on a contract? Megan hesitated before picking it up. This was Cora's bedroom. And she knew Cora's privacy was important to her. But her name was on it. Megan shut the door to Cora's bedroom softly and grabbed the contract, scanning it quickly.

Trevor was a dead man.

Chapter 32

"Hello?" Megan asked into the phone.

"Hi, sweetheart. So how did your bridal shower go? Mom called and said it was a huge success. Too bad about those towels and toasters, huh?"

Megan laughed at the outright lie and hopped up on the counter to get more comfortable.

"Yeah, I'm pretty broken up about it myself. But it was really nice. Your mom was so sweet to put it together for me. And on such short notice too."

"Did your mom decide to come,?" Trevor asked.

Megan closed her eyes, wishing things were different. She had called her mom and personally invited her to the shower, but Trisha had insisted she was way too busy to make it. It was looking like she wasn't in the mood to be involved in any of the wedding preparations.

"Well, she wasn't able to make it this afternoon. But she did say that she might be able to come to lunch at the Tree Room with us."

Trevor frowned, wanting everything to be perfect for Megan. He knew how hard she was working on forgiving her parents. It only seemed right that they do their part. Megan's next question caught him totally off guard though.

"By the way, how did you get your mom to sign your match-making contract? You must really be an amazing negotiator, because if it were me, I'd have held out for more than just a passel of grandkids and a new house."

Trevor sat up in his chair, clutching the phone as if his life depended on it, his voice squeaking like a teenager's.

"You saw the contract!? How did you see it? Did Mom show it to you?"

Megan smiled, leaning back against the wall, enjoying the moment to the fullest.

"Oh, it was just lying around. My only question is, was it really necessary? I mean, I've never known a man who would make his own mother sign a contract to help him secure a wife. I'm really intrigued here."

Trevor walked in a tight circle, rubbing his hand against his forehead, not knowing if her calm voice was camouflaging anger, or if she just thought it was weird. Either way, he wasn't looking too good. If he had only taken his mother's copy with him!

"All I can say is, you were worth any and all effort. I thought I could use all the help I could get, so being the wise businessman that I am, I took advantage of all my resources. As far as making her sign a contract, that was mostly for her benefit. She hates feeling like a burden to me, so she didn't want me paying for a new home for her. This was just my way of making sure that she ends up where she needs to be. Are you okay with this? You're not mad, are you?"

Megan remembered how she had felt just three hours before and was glad he was asking her now, instead of then. If he had been in the same room with her when she had finished reading the contract, she would have shoved her engagement ring down his throat. As luck would have it, she was able to calm down enough to realize that Trevor was just a goof and that sometimes, she actually liked that about him.

"Well, the wedding is still on in case you're worried. But this contract stuff better end right now. I can just see you now, making our children sign contracts about whether or not they brushed their teeth. Let's just go with a little old-fashioned faith and trust, shall we?"

Megan heard Trevor sigh audibly over the phone and

giggled, knowing he had been sweating bullets. They were both getting nervous about their upcoming wedding. Neither one of them wanted to mess it up.

"Megan, I love you."

Megan grinned, closing her eyes and enjoyed the warmth of his feelings.

"I know."

Trevor cleared his throat in irritation. She could be so annoying sometimes.

"Well?"

"Yes, Trevor. I adore you and you know it."

Trevor relaxed finally and sat down, vowing to order the largest bouquet of flowers anyone in Utah had ever seen. He knew she had to work the next day, so he'd have it delivered to her office. She deserved a treat for forgiving him so easily. If the situation had been reversed, he knew he wouldn't have handled it quite so well.

He would just have Blaine do it in the morning. He also needed to send his Mom a copy of a basic prenuptial agreement to look over. She and Drew were getting pretty serious and he wanted his Mom to be protected. He liked Drew all right. Well, not really. But if his mom was in love with the guy, then he'd give him a chance. In the meantime, he'd put as many stumbling blocks in their path as possible. He couldn't think of a bigger stumbling block to married bliss than a pre-nup. He didn't even want to imagine what Megan would have done if he had asked her to sign something so unromantic and heartless. He'd bet their brand new ski lodge he'd just purchased that she would walk out on him. Lucky for him, he was smarter than that.

Chapter 33

Megan drove her El Camino into the parking lot of her office and wondered what Trevor would have waiting for her this day. Every day he had been gone, he had sent her something different. The first day, she had received the cheesiest sweatshirt she had ever seen with their two high school pictures blown up to gruesome proportions. She loved it. She could just picture poor Blaine going to the mall to have that done. She laughed out loud at the picture in her head. But her favorite gift had been the picture of the Timpanogos Temple with the words, "Families are Forever" written underneath in calligraphy. An eternal family was what she wanted more than anything.

Megan opened the door, grinning already in expectation.

"Okay, Jackie, where is it? I know he sent me something. I'm hoping it's chocolates this time. You're not hiding them are you?"

Jackie put her hand on her hip and raised one eyebrow menacingly.

"Excuse me! As if I could use the calories. And no. You didn't get any candy. But UPS delivered something for you a little while ago. That might be from him."

Megan dropped her purse and reached for the envelope. Had he written her a poem? That didn't sound like Trevor, but he could have paid someone to write her one. Hmm. Megan pulled out a legal contract and felt her stomach clench automatically. She had told him no more contracts. Megan scanned the beginning paragraph and went back and read it again more slowly. Trevor had sent her a fill-in-the-blank prenuptial agreement to sign. Without even discussing it with her. How could someone send you a "Families Are Forever" vote of confidence and then a pre-nup the very next day? It was as if he were two different people. He had given her no warning that something like this was even coming.

Megan shoved the papers back into the envelope and rammed it into her briefcase angrily. How dare he do this to her! Jackie had gone to the restroom, so luckily she hadn't been reading over her shoulder. Megan would have died from embarrassment. Now, how to act normal when all she wanted to do was curl up in a ball and cry?

Megan got through her floor time and then drove aimlessly around in her car. She knew Trevor was planning on calling her soon, but she couldn't face talking to him until she had her feelings under control. Besides, what could she say to him? Yes, I realize I am a complete disaster at relationships, but I would still like you to love me enough to overlook that? She'd sound like an idiot. A pathetic idiot.

Megan drove into a parking lot and wasn't surprised to see the familiar temple spires. She locked her doors, turned off her cell phone and leaned her seat back as far as it would go. She had some serious thinking to do. Could she make an eternal commitment to a man who obviously saw her as temporary? The real question was, could she walk out on another wedding? She felt the tears slip down the sides of her cheeks and was only slightly irritated when they started to pool in her ears. As she calmed down enough to pray, she felt an immediate sense of peace and calm fill her body, as if she had plugged into her very own personal space heater. Heavenly Father loved her and wanted her to be happy. But could she be happy with Trevor? An hour and twenty-two minutes later, she had her answer.

Chapter 34

Trevor looked around his empty sky-high condo and smiled. Everything was done. He was pleased that everything had gone so smoothly. Instead of flying to Utah tomorrow as planned, he had changed his ticket to that afternoon. He'd be able to watch the evening news with Megan before she kicked him out. He couldn't wait to see her, although he was a little surprised she hadn't called him to thank him for the bouquet he had sent. Maybe she was just busy with a client. He was certain there was a good reason. Trevor walked over to the window and took one last look out at the Puget Sound before walking out the door. He was ready to return to the mountains, and more than ready for his life with Megan to begin.

* * *

Five hours later, he knocked impatiently on his mother's front door. She would know where Megan was and why she wasn't answering her cell phone. He was starting to worry that something was seriously wrong.

"Trevor! Come on in you darling, darling boy. Let me give you a kiss. No mother ever had a better son than you. Oh I love you."

Trevor walked into his Mom's house smiling, but bewildered. Why had it taken almost thirty years for her to come to that conclusion? He would have sent her a pre-nup contract a long time ago.

"They're so beautiful, I had Drew take my picture by them. I've taken one flower from each variety to press in my scrapbook. Oh, Trev, sometimes I've wondered if you ever really appreciated me, but now I know. You do, you really do. I just hope Megan knows how lucky she is to have you for a husband. You should think of sending her flowers too one of these days."

Trevor's footsteps slowed down as his mother's words sank in. His mother had received flowers from him today. His mother. It would then be logical to assume that Megan had been the one to receive the prenuptial agreement. Trevor stood in front of the largest bouquet he had ever seen in his life and knew he had messed up completely. There would be no forgiveness this time. He was going to kill Blaine. And then he was going to fire him.

Trevor pulled a single red rose from the bouquet and looked at the perfect bud before turning and walking out of his mother's house without saying one word.

Cora followed him to the doorway, baffled by his behavior. She called out to him once, but without turning around, he got in his car and drove away. Cora shrugged and then closed the door. She'd heard jet lag could be exhausting, but this was ridiculous.

Chapter 35

Megan pulled out her last shirt and laid it in the suitcase. It really would be nice to get away for a while. Away from all the stress. Away from problems. She could definitely use a break. Megan grabbed her favorite pair of jeans out of her closet and threw them haphazardly on top of the other clothes she had carelessly packed in her old scuffed up suitcase. The sparkle from her engagement ring caught her eye and made her pause. She frowned as she studied the brilliance of the diamond and the glow of the emeralds. She sighed sadly and went back to packing. It was better to think of other things.

"You didn't answer your door, so I just let myself in. I hope you don't mind."

Megan gasped and turned around, frightened at being surprised.

"What are you doing here?! I didn't think you were coming back until tomorrow."

Trevor's strained face didn't reveal any surprise at seeing Megan's bedroom in an uproar of clothes. It looked as if she were getting ready to make a hasty get away. He didn't blame her one bit.

"I finished early so I thought I'd hurry back. I wanted to see you."

Megan winced at his words and turned her back to grab a dress out of the closet.

"Blaine's been trying to reach you. He called here looking for you about ten minutes ago. He sounded pretty upset."

Trevor's face tightened in anger at the mention of Blaine's name. Blaine was on his own now.

"I believe that's the typical reaction to getting thrown out of your office by Security. I really wish I had been there to see it."

Megan turned around, staring at Trevor in surprise. He and Blaine were like brothers. He would never fire Blaine. Would he?

"You fired Blaine? Why?"

Trevor walked over to Megan's dresser and noticed she had hung her picture of the temple above it. He had known immediately she would love it. He was surprised it wasn't sitting in the trash.

"He made one huge mistake. A mistake that could easily cost me my happiness. He's the one who sent you the prenuptial agreement, Megan. I told him to send it to my mother. I was worried about her relationship with Drew getting serious. You were supposed to get a rather large bouquet of flowers. He switched them. And now my mom is in heaven and you're very, very sad. I can't stand it that you think I would ever have you sign anything like that. That I would want you to."

Megan sat down on her bed, crossing her arms over her knees. Blaine had sent her the contract?

"Are you saying this was all a mix-up? An accident?"

Trevor felt a tremor of hope enter his heart, as he heard the doubt in Megan's voice. Maybe it was possible to talk his way out of this one. He said a silent prayer and crossed his fingers.

"Yes. In the biggest way."

Megan looked suspiciously over at Trevor, her eyes narrowed.

"Trevor, I don't know if I can believe you. I've seen plenty of evidence just in the past month alone that proves you like to manipulate people, bribe people, twist people around until they do what you want them to. How do I know this wasn't some sick scheme or test to make sure I wasn't marrying you for your money?"

Trevor sighed, his hope gone. The marriage was off. He knew it.

"Because I have faith in you. I wish you had a little in me."

Trevor turned and walked towards the door, and out of Megan's life.

Whack!

Trevor felt something hit him squarely in the back of the head and turned around in surprise. He hadn't realized Megan had a violent side. On the floor where it had fallen lay the prenuptial agreement. Trevor picked it up, just in case he ever ran into Blaine again. He would shove it in his face and demand a duel. Or something.

"Read it, you knothead," Megan said as she sat down in a chair.

Trevor smoothed out the paper, wondering what horrible obscenities she had plastered on it and was surprised to see nothing. Nothing except a small signature at the bottom. She had signed the prenuptial agreement. She would have married him anyway. She was still planning on marrying him!

Megan felt tears slide down her face at Trevor's look of awe. For once in her life, she had kept the faith. Trevor said nothing as he ripped up the contract and walked over to kneel in front of Megan, resting his head on her knees.

"I wasn't kidding when I said I loved you. I actually meant it," Megan said softly into his hair.

Trevor sighed deeply, overcome and humbled by the gift she had given him. Something much more precious than money. Her heart. Trevor lifted his head and got up from the floor and held out his hand. Megan wiped her eyes and took his hand. He pulled her gently to her feet and then cupped her face in his hands, leaning down to kiss her once on her forehead, then on both cheeks and then pulled her into his arms.

"I love you, Megan."

Megan felt the tenseness of Trevor's muscles relax as he continued to hug her and smiled for the first time in almost nine hours. Love was a miracle. Megan tilted her head up and kissed Trevor on the chin to get his attention.

"And I want you to forgive Blaine. It was a simple mistake."

Anything except that. He would never forgive Blaine. He still wanted to kill Blaine. He wanted to throw rotten fruit at Blaine. He wanted to run over Blaine's new car with a tank. He wanted to see Blaine eat the prenuptial agreement he had ripped into pieces.

"Why don't we talk about something else? Like, why you told me you were so good at packing?"

Megan laughed and hugged Trevor one last time before pulling out of his arms.

"So sue me, I was under pressure. You try coming up with ten good qualities in under a minute. Hold on, you're trying to change the subject on me."

Trevor grabbed Megan by the hand and pulled her out of her room and towards the front door.

"Hey! Where are you taking me? I still have to finish packing for our honeymoon."

Trevor pulled her out the front door and had her in his car before answering.

"I'm taking you to see the world's largest bouquet of flowers. They were supposed to be yours but my mom got them instead. You've got to see it, but don't burst her bubble. It takes up Mom's whole living room it's so huge."

Megan laughed as she relaxed back into the leather seat and felt all of the tension ease out of her body. Heavenly Father was right after all. Trust and love do go hand in hand.

"I want you to forgive Blaine. I kind of even want you to rehire him. It would make a really nice wedding present."

Trevor thought of the ski lodge he had just bought her for a wedding present and begged to differ.

"Never."

Megan blew the hair out of her eyes in irritation. He was being really stubborn about this.

"If I can forgive you all of your horrendous blunders, don't you think you can forgive Blaine, one small mistake?"

Trevor's black eyes snapped in anger and his hands tightened on the steering wheel.

"Small? No. That was an enormous mistake. Admit it. When you saw that pre-nup, the first thing you thought of doing was dumping me. Try and deny it."

Megan looked out the window, knowing her guilt was very apparent.

"Well, that's why I'm an adult. I think things through. I don't make life-changing decisions on a moment's anger. And neither should you. Besides, wasn't it you who gave me a little speech about the Atonement and how we're supposed to forgive everybody, everything? You wouldn't want me to think you're a hypocrite would you?"

Trevor groaned and shook his head.

"But I already got you a wedding present."

Megan reached over and held Trevor's hand between the seats. He was such a little kid.

"So give me two."

Trevor didn't want to tell her she was getting approximately three hundred. It would ruin the surprise.

"I hope you're not going to be disappointed, but I spent practically every last cent I had on your wedding ring. I feel bad, but I don't have a wedding present for you."

Trevor raised Megan's hand to his mouth and smiled.

"You already gave me the best wedding present there is. A trusting heart."

And it was true.

Epilogue

Saturday morning Trevor led Megan into the sealing room. He helped her to kneel on her side of the altar and then walked around to kneel across from her.

Megan looked contentedly around the small room at the few precious people they had invited to be there with them. Cora was the only parent there to support them. Linette was waiting for them outside in the gardens. Blaine and Drew were the witnesses. Heartbreakingly absent were her parents.

After the ceremony, Brother Perry, their sealer, instructed them to kiss across the altar. Trevor leaned over and took her face in his hands, smiling down into her eyes with the sweetest expression she had ever seen. He loved her and he couldn't be telling her more eloquently. He leaned down and pressed his mouth gently across hers in a pure and chaste expression of his commitment to her. She closed her eyes and accepted him. As Trevor pulled away, he kept his eyes locked on hers, letting her know that their covenant was sealed with love.

Her heart had been broken in so many different ways, by Dylan and Taffie and by her parents. But it had been broken in such a way that true love had been able to enter in. Trevor reached for her hand and raised her from her knees. As he led her out of the sealing room and into their new life together, she knew she would keep this moment in her heart forever. And because families are forever, she knew she could.

About the Author

In the fourth grade, Shannon Guymon wandered into the school library and figuratively never came out again. She decided one day to take her love affair with the written word once step further, and wrote her first novel, *Never Letting Go of Hope*.

A Trusting Heart is her second novel.

Shannon grew up all across the United States, but has finally found her home in Alpine, Utah, where she lives with her four children and her husband Matt. She enjoys the mountains, gardening, being with her family, and of course, writing.